GHOULFRIENDS

who's that ghoulfriend?

ALSO BY
GITTY DANESHVARI

Ghoulfriends Forever

Ghoulfriends Just Want to Have Fun

School of Fear

School of Fear: Class Is NOT Dismissed!

School of Fear: The Final Exam

GHOULFRIENDS
who's that ghoulfriend?

WRITTEN BY
GITTY DANESHVARI

ILLUSTRATED BY
DARKO DORDEVIC

LITTLE, BROWN AND COMPANY
NEW YORK • BOSTON

Spot art by Chuck Gonzales

This book is a work of fiction. Names, characters, places, and incidents are the product of the author's imagination or are used fictitiously. Any resemblance to actual events, locales, or persons, living or dead, is coincidental.

Little, Brown and Company

Hachette Book Group
237 Park Avenue, New York, NY 10017
Visit our website at www.lb-kids.com

Little, Brown and Company is a division of
Hachette Book Group, Inc.
The Little, Brown name and logo
are trademarks of Hachette Book Group, Inc.

The publisher is not responsible for websites (or their content) that are not owned by the publisher.

First Edition: September 2013

Library of Congress Control Number: 2013015031

ISBN 978-0-316-22254-9

10 9 8 7 6 5 4 3 2 1

RRD-C

Printed in the United States of America

For the original Miss Stein—Erin.
Thank you for your inexhaustible
patience and encouragement.

CHAPTER one

Wax splashed softly against the cold stone floor as six fashionably clad feet tiptoed along a candlelit corridor. Left, right, left, right—the rot-iron heels, copper boots, and wedge sneakers moved in military-like unison. Quiet but for the faint sounds of a storm raging outside, an eerie tension gripped the space. Flames flickered fitfully, condensation clung to the windows, and the unmistakable scent of staleness flourished. A smooth green hand emerged from the darkness, grabbed hold of a tarnished brass

1

doorknob, and pulled. High-pitched squeals erupted from the rusted hinges as the attic door opened, revealing a dark stairwell.

"Whether by fate or by choice, ever since our arrival at Monster High, we've found ourselves protecting the school. But tonight I think we can all agree that the stakes have been raised," Venus McFlytrap, the daughter of the plant monster, said somberly, her jade complexion and bright pink-and-green hair shimmering in the candlelight. "So before we go up there, I just want to know one thing. Are you ready?"

"For clarification's sake, when you ask if we're ready, are you referring to finding Headmistress Bloodgood, thwarting the anonymous forces wishing to control Monster High, or confronting the spider ghoul in the attic?" Rochelle Goyle, a

petite gargoyle from Scaris, inquired in her usual formal manner.

"I'm pretty sure they're all connected . . . somehow. But seeing as we're seconds away from heading into the attic, I'd say the spider ghoul is the most important," Venus responded as the vines around her arms bristled with nervous anticipation.

"Spider ghouls have always fascinated me. With six hands they are natural multitaskers. They can simultaneously brush their hair, floss their teeth, apply makeup, type an e-mail, carry a handbag, and pet the dog. If you ask me, it's *très* impressive," Rochelle said as she lifted one of her granite hands in the air. "Of course, having said that, depending on the spider ghoul's disposition, six hands could also make

3

her a very lively adversary. She could literally throw a stapler, a Casketball, a book, a lamp, an iCoffin, and a shoe at us—all at the same time."

"Bottom line, Rochelle, yes or no?" Venus tried to make her loquacious friend focus.

"Yes," Rochelle replied as she pulled her long pink mane with teal streaks into a bun, showcasing her small stone wings in the process. "By the way, paragraph 13.3 of the Gargoyle Code of Ethics clearly states that when in the company of candles, long-haired ghouls must pull their hair back to avoid follicular fires."

"I'll be sure to try and remember that," Venus said carefully before turning to Robecca Steam, a beautiful blue-and-black-haired ghoul crafted from a copper steam engine by her

4

mad-scientist father. "What about you, Becs? Are you ready?"

"You needn't worry if you didn't bring the proper hair accessories. I always carry extra rubber bands and scarves," Rochelle interrupted. "They may not match your outfits, but as we say in Scaris, *la securité avant la mode*, safety before fashion!"

"Thank you, Rochelle," Venus barked dismissively, and then raised her eyebrows at Robecca. "Well?"

"Of course, ideally, one would have both safety *and* fashion," Rochelle once again interjected.

"Rochelle! Enough about candles and hair and fashion! In case you haven't noticed I'm trying to talk to Robecca!" Venus exploded in exasperation.

"*Boo-la-la*, no need to get your pollens pumping. I was only trying to help," Rochelle

5

chastised Venus, who promptly rolled her eyes in response.

"So, Becs? Are you ready?" Venus once again asked her friend.

"Jeepers creepers! *Ready* feels like an awfully strong word. I think *sort of ready* or *kind of ready* is more appropriate," Robecca babbled as small clouds of steam puffed from her copper-covered ears.

"Robecca, if you cannot accompany us to the attic, you needn't worry. Venus and I can handle it," Rochelle explained calmly. "Or, to be precise, I am sixty-eight to seventy-five percent certain that we can handle it."

"Sometimes I think you just make all these statistics up," Venus mumbled under her breath.

"*Ce n'est pas vrai!* A gargoyle is nothing if

not honest with her statistics," Rochelle huffed, and then grabbed Robecca's warm metallic arm. "Now then, we shouldn't be gone too long."

"Oh no! You misunderstood me," said Robecca. "I might not be ready, but I'm definitely coming with you ghouls. How could I not? We're Headmistress Bloodgood's only chance!"

So much had happened in the short time that Robecca, Rochelle, and Venus had been at Monster High. Why, only the semester before, the threesome had battled the Whisper, a powerful spell that robbed students and teachers alike of their ability to think for themselves. And though the perpetrator of the Whisper, Miss Flapper, claimed to have been under a spell as well, the threesome remained unconvinced of her innocence. However, they were the only ones.

By the start of the following semester, it had appeared as though everyone at Monster High had forgotten about Miss Flapper using the Whisper to control the school. Even the appearance of dolls of doom and fluffy white cats—traditionally considered signs of bad luck—hardly elicited a response from the student body. In fact, it was not until the arrival of notes and graffiti warning of an ominous "them" that alarms were sounded. Yet even so, Miss Flapper continued to avoid the shadow of suspicion. At least until tonight . . .

High winds, pounding rain, and splintering strands of lightning had barreled through Salem, knocking out the power and stranding students and staff on the Monster High campus. Eager to keep her captive campers entertained, Headmistress Bloodgood had allowed the Hex Factor Talon

Show to go on as planned. However, at 9 PM sharp, the show took a most unexpected turn when a DeadEx zombie arrived. The slow-moving courier delivered a letter, which shortly thereafter was read to the student body and teachers: Headmistress Bloodgood had been taken by normies and would not be returned until a wall was erected around Salem—effectively imprisoning the town!

As fear and anxiety swept through the school, blogger Spectra Vondergeist had made a shocking confession to Robecca, Rochelle, and Venus. Having spotted Miss Flapper sneaking into the attic on numerous occasions, the violet-haired ghost had decided to check out the oft-forgotten space for herself. And though Spectra hadn't a clue what to expect, she was rather surprised to find a slumbering spider ghoul up there.

The sound of shuffling feet captured the ghouls' attention, instantly waking them from their recollections of the events earlier that evening.

"Hey," a soft male voice called out.

Cy Clops, a tall and lanky boy, stepped into the faint pool of light cast by Robecca's, Rochelle's, and Venus's candles. With his shoulders slightly hunched, the naturally timid Cyclops flashed his friends and dormmates a quick smile. Having weathered the Whisper and its aftermath with the trio, Cy had more than proven himself a trustworthy friend.

"Oh, Cy! You're here!" Robecca squealed happily as she threw one arm around the one-eyed boy's shoulders and squeezed.

Cy's normally alabaster cheeks turned pink at the touch of his faithful crush Robecca.

"I hardly think this reunion warrants so much enthusiasm. You only left Cy ten minutes ago," Venus remarked wryly to Robecca.

"Cy, were you able to locate Madame Flapper?" Rochelle inquired as she tapped her granite claws against the base of her candle.

Bits of wax splattered about haphazardly, prompting Cy to crouch down and cover his face with his hands.

"Sorry, but when you have an eye as big as I do, you worry about things getting into it."

"Ah! *Je suis desolée!* It's one of my most irksome goylisms. I tap my claws without even realizing that I'm doing it," Rochelle apologized.

"It's okay," Cy replied as he stood up straight. "And as for Miss Flapper, she's in the Creepateria with Jinafire and Skelita."

Jinafire Long, a dragon from Fanghai, and Skelita Calaveras, a *calaca* from Hexico, had been lured in by Miss Flapper's charms immediately upon arriving at Monster High. Robecca, Rochelle, and Venus couldn't quite tell whether they simply idolized the fashion-savvy teacher or were in the throes of something more sinister, like a spell.

"Jinafire and Skelita are both pretty freaked out about the so-called normie invasion, so I doubt Miss Flapper will be going anywhere for a while," Cy finished.

"It's almost midnight," Venus said after looking at her watch. "So I think it's time to head up these stairs," she continued before starting up the stone-walled passageway.

Littered haphazardly along the edge of the steps was an odd array of school paraphernalia,

12

everything from trophies to outdated microscopes to deflated Casketballs. However, unlike most items stashed away in unused corridors, these were not covered in dust but rather in smooth and shimmery strands.

"At least we finally know where all the spiderwebs are coming from," Venus remarked, surveying the surroundings.

"I always thought it was *trés* bizarre that for all the webs we see on campus we hardly see any spiders, outside of the small cluster in the dormitory, that is," Rochelle added.

"And don't forget that some of the dolls of doom and notes had spider threads on them," Robecca squeaked, shaking her head nervously. "Jeez Louise, is high school always going to be this stressful?"

"The spider ghoul is clearly involved with what's been happening on campus. But the question remains, who is she working for and what are they ultimately after . . . ?" Venus trailed off in frustration.

"Well, obviously she's working with Miss Flapper, since Spectra saw her coming up here," Cy responded in his usual soft-spoken way.

"Yeah, but do we really think it's just the two of them?" Venus countered.

"Um, Venus?" Robecca stuttered nervously as they ascended the stairs.

"Yes?"

"You know I hate to be pushy, but what exactly is the plan here? Are we simply going to introduce ourselves to the spider ghoul and inquire what she's doing at Monster High? How she knows Miss

Flapper? Why she left notes, graffiti, and dolls all over campus?" Robecca babbled rapidly, without stopping to take so much as a breath between words.

"Technically speaking, I don't actually have a *plan*," Venus replied slowly, laboring over each word as though that would make the information more palatable.

"*Pardonnez-moi*? What was that you said?" Rochelle called out from farther down the stairs.

"I said I don't have a plan, or at least not a formal one," Venus admitted grudgingly.

"Paragraph 80.7 of the Gargoyle Code of Ethics maintains that mission leaders must have a plan before beginning the task. Therefore, I vote we pause our activity, formulate a plan, and then

reengage," Rochelle explained, her voice growing louder as she caught up to Venus.

"How long is the Gargoyle Code of Ethics? Because it's beginning to feel like there's a section on everything from flossing your teeth to breathing," Venus grumbled.

"It's 1,714 pages long. And yes, there are sections on both flossing and breathing," Rochelle retorted. "Now about the plan, should we stop and write something down? I just so happen to have both a pen and piece of paper on me, not to mention excellent handwriting."

"Write something down? You can't be serious?" Venus moaned.

"Gargoyles are always serious, or haven't you heard?" Cy mumbled under his breath.

"What if the spider ghoul gets angry? After all,

we are barging in on her unannounced," Robecca worried aloud. "What if she knows a martial art? I heard spiders are naturals at goo-jitsu!"

"Goo-jitsu? Where on earth is this coming from?" Venus blustered.

"She has six arms! How will I protect . . . ?" Robecca paused and then gasped, having just remembered her mechanical pet penguin. "Penny! Where have I left her this time? I hope not the washing machine again. All that spinning gave her such a headache."

"Penny is in your dorm room along with Roux and Chewy," Cy reassured Robecca, while pondering what a funny trio the pets made.

The always-hungry houseplant Chewlian, per-petually happy griffin Roux, and the eternally grumpy mechanical penguin Penny definitely made

an interesting group. But then again, just look at their owners.

"Listen up, ghouls . . . and guy. I know this is scary, but if this spider ghoul has anything to do with Headmistress Bloodgood's disappearance, and I think we all suspect she does, then there's no time to lose," Venus explained as the stairs came to an end before a wall of webbed curtains.

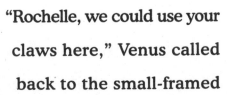

Intricate designs containing the school crest, birds, and vines adorned each of the silky sheaths covering the entryway to the attic.

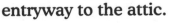

"Rochelle, we could use your claws here," Venus called back to the small-framed

gargoyle, after noting the stickiness of the webs.

"Shouldn't we knock or ring the doorbell or something?" Robecca mumbled anxiously while fiddling with her sapphire-hued hair.

"First of all, there's no doorbell; it's an attic. And second of all, you can't knock on spider-webs," Venus explained logically.

"Deary me, this situation really has put a bee in my bonnet, because now my head won't stop buzzing," Robecca whined.

As the sharp-clawed Rochelle sliced through the weaving, she winced with pain. So exquisite were the designs that she thought them more spooktacular than anything she'd seen in Scaremès or Croako Chanel. And that said something, for Rochelle absolutely adored both fashion houses.

Following a few minutes of meticulous work,

Rochelle made her way through the newly carved opening in the sheaths.

"Do you see her?" Venus whispered to Rochelle as she disappeared from view.

Five long seconds passed without a sound.

"Rochelle? Are you okay?" the plant ghoul called out in an unusually high-pitched voice, adrenaline surging through her thick green veins.

But again there was no response.

CHAPTER two

n all my years, I have never seen such beauty and fine craftsmanship," Rochelle babbled, her eyes glazed over with wonder, as the others barreled into the room behind her.

"In the name of flora and fauna, you scared me!" Venus huffed as she and the others blew out their candles. "You couldn't just have said that the spider ghoul wasn't here? Or that you were okay?"

"Wow! This place is fangtastic!" Robecca proclaimed loudly, her hazel eyes widening to take in the sights.

Dangling from exposed beams, an array of webbed lanterns bathed the room in warm candlelight. Small, delicately crafted snowflakes decorated the walls, creating both a wondrous and wintry effect. And smack-dab in the middle of the room was a fluffy banana-shaped hammock, which seemed to invite all who saw it to take a nap. Long and billowy curtains, a tightly knit rug, and a wardrobe filled out the rest of the enchanting loftlike space.

"This ghoul is clearly an incredible talent. An absolute genius," Rochelle marveled. "Just think what Clawdeen could create with this material!"

Silky-maned werewolf Clawdeen Wolf was the school's foremost designer, not to mention the latest winner of the prestigious Moanatella Ghostier Fashion Fellowship.

"Um, hello?" Venus exclaimed with palpable irritation. "The spider ghoul's also working with Miss Flapper. And most likely involved with Headmistress Bloodgood's kidnapping."

"Venus is right. Whether she's talented or not shouldn't change anything," Cy muttered in agreement.

"*Boo-la-la*, I cannot believe I allowed myself to be swayed by finely woven fabrics and captivating designs. The fact that she created this boo-tiful space is completely irrelevant," Rochelle admitted with a hint of embarrassment.

The granite ghoul then lowered her head and silently smarted over her ability to be distracted at such a turbulent time. It was behavior not only unbecoming to a gargoyle but downright irresponsible. After all, Headmistress Bloodgood

was missing, and what could be more important than that? Well, maybe a few things, but certainly not fabrics.

"Someone's got a bit of a glove addiction," Venus surmised as she looked through the spider ghoul's wardrobe for clues.

"In fairness, she does have six hands," Cy responded as he pulled back the floor-to-ceiling curtains and looked out the small window at Monster High's front lawn. "The storm seems to have passed, so hopefully the power will be back on soon."

"Thank heavens! I can only imagine the nibbling Penny and Roux are being subjected to by Chewy. That plant can barely see even when the lights are on," Robecca babbled as her knees began to squeak.

26

"What can I say? He's a got an insatiable appetite and poor vision. Admittedly, it's not the best combination," Venus replied. "Oh, and, Robecca? I think it may be time for an oil change at Grind 'n' Gears. Unless, of course, you like sounding like an old furnace."

"An old furnace?! Heavens to Betsy! What could be worse?"

"Being disassembled again, sharing a toothbrush with a troll, having a piano land on your foot, sharing a hairbrush with a troll, rust, an empty boiler," Rochelle answered seriously, and then paused. "You weren't actually asking, were you?"

"No, but I still appreciate the information. It helps keep things in perspective," Robecca responded, stifling laughter.

Still standing in front of the small window, Cy spotted something at the far end of the ledge. It appeared to be a crumpled receipt, but he couldn't say for sure. Rather surprisingly, given the sheer size of their eyes, Cyclopes had notoriously poor vision. In fact, according to the Encyclopedia, the island of Cyclopes strictly forbade its inhabitants to drive motorized vehicles, use industrial machinery, or act as eyewitnesses in legal proceedings.

Curious, Cy stepped closer to the far end of the windowsill, which brought a crumpled photograph of a castle into focus. The large stone fortress with gothic arches, turrets, and a moat instantly ignited a memory in the one-eyed boy. Earlier that semester in Monstory, the class had studied architecture of the Old World, the land

across the ocean, and this was definitely it. There simply weren't buildings like this in the New World, or as it was informally known, the "Boo World."

After staring at the photograph for a few seconds, Cy turned it over and saw a clumsily scrawled message: *Wydowna, never forget where you come from or whom you serve.*

"Ghouls, I think you're going to want to see this," Cy stated ominously, instantly inciting the interest of Robecca, Rochelle, and Venus, who hurried over to check out the photograph.

"'Wydowna' is her name," Rochelle muttered while reading the back of the picture. "Well, it certainly explains all the monogrammed Ws on her clothing."

"'Never forget where you come from or *whom*

you serve,'" Robecca repeated aloud. "I don't like the sound of that . . . unless of course she's a waitress."

"Becs," Venus said with a sigh.

"Wishful thinking?" Robecca muttered.

"You could say that," Venus replied drily.

"Did anyone notice there's a panel missing from the wall?" Rochelle asked as she crossed the room and peered inside the exposed crawl space.

"Now we know who visited Miss Flapper," Venus stated, referring to the ghoul they heard traipsing across their ceiling and then descending into Miss Flapper's room.

"In light of the message on this photograph, I think it wise we finish searching the room and get out of here as soon as possible. It's to our advantage that Wydowna, Madame Flapper, and

whomever they're *serving* don't know we're onto them," Rochelle explained to the others.

"I agree; having them on our tail will only make finding Headmistress Bloodgood more difficult," Cy remarked.

"Well, there's nowhere left to look anyway, except maybe under the carpet," Venus said as she bent down and pushed back the rug.

The faint sound of scuffling began to emanate from the crawl space. And though it was a soft and muffled noise, it instantly grabbed the foursome's attention. Adrenaline rushed through their bodies as they exchanged tense expressions. Venus immediately put back the rug and tried to stand. But she couldn't. One of the thick green vines that grew out of her arms was wedged between the floorboards.

"I'm stuck," Venus hissed, frantically pulling at her vine.

"Plant down! Plant down!" Robecca cried in alarm, steam pouring out of her nostrils.

"*Quel désastre*! Steam and webs do not mix. Or rather, when they do it becomes like glue," Rochelle explained, feverishly tapping her claws against her cheek.

"Come on," Cy said as he threw his sweater over Robecca's face and pulled her back toward the path to the stairs.

"We can't leave Venus. We have a no-plant-left-behind policy," Robecca mumbled from beneath the fabric while the sounds of the spider ghoul approaching grew louder.

"Rochelle's helping her," Cy whispered as the two disappeared from view.

"*S'il ghoul plaît*, Venus, you must relax," Rochelle said calmly, attempting to maneuver the vine out from between two planks of wood.

"It's hard to relax when I can hear her coming," Venus murmured as the distinctive scrambling sounds from the crawl space continued to increase in volume.

"Almost got it," Rochelle said through gritted teeth.

Seconds later Rochelle lifted a plank of wood from the floor, freeing Venus's vine and exposing a cache of hidden papers.

"I never thought there could be an upside to getting a vine stuck, but clearly I was wrong," Venus mumbled, a smile creeping across her face.

"While I admit your vine getting stuck has proven advantageous, may I remind you that

33

the spider ghoul is just about here?" Rochelle whispered, keeping her eyes trained on the crawl space across the room.

Venus whipped her head around to look at the opening in the wall and then nodded at Rochelle.

"You're right. There isn't time to read these papers now."

"Exactly! *Allez-y!*" Rochelle said as she gripped Venus's green arm and attempted to stand.

"Not yet," Venus replied brusquely as she pulled out her iCoffin and began snapping photos of the documents.

"*Je suis tellement serieuse!* We must go right now," Rochelle implored. "Wydowna is just about here."

"Just a sec, I'm almost done."

"*C'est trop tard*, Venus. It's too late," Rochelle

34

uttered faintly as she heard the distinct sound of a creature crawling into the room.

Venus dropped the papers and silently pushed the floorboard back in place. She then turned toward Rochelle and shook her head as if to say, "I'm sorry, I didn't listen." For though they were momentarily concealed by the dimness of the room, discovery was only a matter of time. Anxious anticipation overwhelmed the ghouls, leaving them with tightened chests and mouths as dry as mummy wrappings. After quickly assessing the options, Venus decided it best she announce their presence to Wydowna. However, just as she started to move, Rochelle grabbed her hand and pulled her to the floor. The granite ghoul then draped the long and billowy curtain from the nearby window over them. And though this

hiding spot was hardly deft, the faint lighting did wonders for their disguise.

After Wydowna lit a couple of additional candles, Venus and Rochelle were able to catch a glimpse of her, albeit through the gauzy curtain. Sleek and slender with pitch-black skin and long flame-colored locks, Wydowna was a ghoul few could forget. And not simply because she had six arms and six eyes, four of which simply looked like teardrop-shaped swaths of red on her forehead. Dressed in black knee-high boots and a slinky webbed dress dyed the same shade as her hair, Wydowna's style was the perfect mixture of strength and femininity.

"Where are you?" Wydowna purred, sending chills up the ghouls' spines. "There's no point hiding. I know you're in here."

Venus and Rochelle held their breaths and closed their eyes, unsure how to handle the situation. How did Wydowna know they were in there, but not where they were hiding? Could she smell them? Or was it something else? Was it a spider sense?

"You don't want my fangs to fill with venom, do you?" Wydowna asked in a frighteningly calm manner as she made her way toward the ghouls.

Venom?! Venom!? Venom?!

The word echoed in Venus's and Rochelle's minds as they pondered the catastrophic effects the spider's serum could have on both plants and stones.

CHAPTER
three

istening to Wydowna's boots knock against the wooden floor resigned Rochelle and Venus to their fate. There was simply no way around it; the spider ghoul was about to lift the curtain. And once she did, it would only be a matter of time until Miss Flapper was informed and the search for Headmistress Bloodgood grew even more complex.

"There you are! You silly ghoul!" Wydowna gushed, her voice now overflowing with warmth and affection.

Seconds later, a soft buzzing sound filled the

air as two translucent wings flapped past Rochelle and Venus. It came as quite a surprise since neither ghoul had noticed a cat-size fly with a red bow atop its head and a shiny rhinestone collar around its neck when they inspected the room. And frankly, that's a hard thing to miss. But, in their defense, flies were rather adept at hiding in rafters and other hard-to-reach places.

"What were you doing up in the corner, Shoo? Playing hide-and-screech by yourself again?" Wydowna asked, cradling the creature in her arms. "What's the matter? Why are you shaking?"

However illogical, both Venus and Rochelle momentarily worried that they might be able to communicate nonverbally with each other, and that Shoo could convey their presence to Wydowna telepathically. But of course, neither

40

one of the ghouls knew very much about spiders or flies, a fact that greatly bothered Rochelle. As a gargoyle, she found lacking knowledge to be a most irksome state of mind.

"Did Miss Flapper stop by again? I know how she scares you," Wydowna said as she dropped her pet fly into the hammock and began weaving something. "Just a minute, Shoo, I'm almost done. Although, why you insist on fresh pajamas nightly I'll never understand."

Watching from beneath the meshlike curtain, Rochelle once again felt pangs of awe. Not for the ghoul herself, but for her talent. After all, it was hardly a secret that Rochelle yearned to be able to create her own couture clothing. In fact, the mere thought of it gave her granite skin goose bumps. Instantly enraptured in a fashionable reverie,

Rochelle didn't even notice Venus's deep frown over Shoo's wastefulness. Never mind that spider webs were biodegradable; Venus believed it set an environmentally reckless precedent to wear new pajamas every night.

"Good night, Shoo," Wydowna cooed as she joined her pet fly in the hammock.

Unbeknownst to Venus and Rochelle, spiders took a very long time to fall asleep. But then again, maneuvering eight limbs into a comfortable position was quite an undertaking. Toss, turn, move arm one, turn again, rotate arm three, toss once more, adjust arm four, and on and on it went. So lengthy was the process that Rochelle and Venus had almost fallen asleep by the time they heard the telltale sounds of slumber. Eager to leave, the ghouls quickly crawled out from

beneath the curtain, stood up, and started for the exit. Only a few steps in, Venus got the distinct sensation that she was being watched. Her leaves instantly stood on end and her pollens began to pump as she turned slowly toward the hammock.

Two small and beady eyes, the color of mustard, met Venus's gaze. Worried Shoo might try to wake Wydowna, Venus quickly pushed Rochelle through the sheaths and into the stairwell.

Once out of the attic, the bleary-eyed ghouls engaged in some serious stretching. Remaining perfectly still for so many hours had left them rather stiff. Venus and Rochelle then looked at their watches, their eyes widening in disbelief. It was six AM. Suddenly eager to find their friends, the two quickly hurried down the steps.

"I'm sure glad they weren't up all night

43

worrying about us," Venus remarked playfully at the sight of Cy and Robecca slouched over, fast asleep, halfway down the stairs.

"If it makes you feel better, I doubt they're well rested. You soft-bodied monsters lack the durability to sleep soundly on stone," Rochelle explained, bending down to tap Robecca on the shoulder.

"What time is it? What time is it?" Robecca rambled, still half asleep. "Where's Penny? What is this place? Have I been sleepwalking again?"

"We're in the stairwell to the attic. We came here late last night to see the spider ghoul," Cy reminded Robecca as he wiped the sleep from his eye.

"Oh yes, that's right; we found out her name is Wydowna and that she's serving someone," Robecca said with a knowing look, before turning

toward Rochelle and Venus. "Sorry we nodded off. Are you okay? You both look seriously tired. I'm guessing that means you weren't able to grab any shut-eye while hiding in the attic."

"Not a wink," Venus responded gruffly.

"Technically speaking, that is not accurate. We did in fact experience quite a few winks, however, we were awake for them," Rochelle clarified before raising one eyebrow. "Like all gargoyles, I yearn for the day that misleading colloquialisms are outlawed."

"But what about free speech?" Robecca asked.

"What about it? There's nothing free about confusing and occasionally even deceptive sayings," Rochelle retorted.

"Ghouls, I'm sorry, but the free-speech discussion is going to have to wait. We need to

head over to the main corridor and see what's happening," Venus asserted as she started down the stone steps.

The purple checkered floor and pink coffin-shaped lockers in the main hall were barely visible because of the dense crowd of monsters crammed into the space. Parents, teachers, and students swarmed an unidentified man and woman, above whom a sea of bats slept peacefully in the rafters, blissfully unaware of the pandemonium below.

"I think it's *très* important that we identify the people at the center of this commotion *tout de suite*," Rochelle stated, turning toward Venus. "So in the name of efficiency, please use your innate pushiness to get us to the front of the crowd."

"Excuse me, but I am not pushy," Venus clarified.

"*Boo-la-la*, Venus, *ce n'est pas un secret*. Everyone knows that you're pushy. There's no point denying it."

"Sorry, Rochelle, but you're wrong about this one. Right, Becs?" Venus implored her copper-plated friend.

"Talk about being stuck between a plant and a hard place," Robecca prattled, her eyes flitting back and forth between her two ghoulfriends.

"May I remind you that paragraph 12.3 of the Gargoyle Code of Ethics states that true friendship requires honesty?"

"Venus is pushy," Robecca muttered quickly, her eyes trained on the floor.

"You ghouls are just overly sensitive. Cy knows—" Venus said, turning toward the quiet one-eyed boy.

"You're pushy," Cy interrupted, eager to bring the debate to an end. "And I hope you can forgive me for saying as much."

"Yes, me too, Venus. You know how much I adore you—all of you, even your pushiness," Rochelle added.

"Fine, but for future reference I prefer the term *assertive*," Venus remarked as she forcibly inserted herself into the crowd.

The assembled group of concerned parents, unnerved teachers, and confused students emitted a collective air of hysteria. Furrowed brows, sweaty palms, and chattering fangs swept through the crowd as everyone struggled to come to terms with a missing headmistress and a potential normie threat.

"Move it, please," Venus said as she pushed

past a monster drinking a Croak-a-Cola. "It's kind of early for soda, isn't it? Oh, and don't forget to recycle the can when you're done."

"I think *excuse me* is a more appropriate phrase than *move it, n'est-ce pas*?" Rochelle whispered to Cy and Robecca.

"I wouldn't say anything if I were you. You know how grumpy plants are when they haven't slept," Cy advised Rochelle as they came to the center of the crowd.

A row of filthy-faced trolls, each greasier and more unattractive than the next, stood guard over a zombie and a mummy, both of whom had their backs pressed against the wall.

"I recognize them from the local paper. The zombie's Scariff Fred Onarrival and the mummy is Skultastic Superintendent Petra Fied,"

Rochelle leaned in and whispered to the others.

Scariff Fred was a stout zombie with an ample belly, bloodshot eyes, and a receding hairline. While by no means attractive, the scariff exuded an air of power and control. As did the tall and stern-looking mummy standing next to him, Superintendent Petra.

"Excuse me, may we have your attention?" Scariff Fred said, speaking into a special bullhorn that translated Zombese into English.

The trolls standing before the scariff and superintendent then stepped threateningly toward the crowd.

"You listen now! No talk! Only listen!" the trolls screamed while wagging their dirty sausage-shaped fingers at the mass of students, parents, and teachers.

"*Quelle horreur*," Rochelle lamented at the sight of the stout beasts' filthy hands. "I will never understand why hygiene remains such a foreign concept to them."

"Thank you, trolls, that's quite enough," Scariff Fred said as he looked out at the sea of concerned faces. "Superintendent Petra and I would like you all to know that we're doing everything in our power to keep the students safe and bring Headmistress Bloodgood home. And while these bullies, the normies, may think they can intimidate us into walling ourselves off—they're wrong, dead wrong."

Venus's vines quivered, Robecca's rivets rattled, and Rochelle's claws rapped as they reflected on the scariff's unsettling comments. They simply could not understand why everyone so

easily accepted the letter at face value. Surely the scariff knew that dubious forces often used forgery as a means of getting what they wanted.

"Excuse me, scariff?" Venus blurted out, suddenly overwhelmed by a desire to question his belief in the normie story.

"*Boo alors*, what are you doing, Venus?"

"It's not too late; just ask for the time," Robecca advised, small balls of steam exiting her ears. "That's what I do, but then again I never know the time."

"Yes, ghoul?" the scariff responded, looking directly at Venus.

"How do you know it was really the normies who took Headmistress Bloodgood? After all, any monster could have written that letter," Venus pointed out logically.

52

"Children should not question their elders unless specifically instructed to do so," Superintendent Petra grumbled, with all but her lips remaining eerily still.

"It's all right, Petra," the scariff replied before turning toward Venus and assuming a decidedly patronizing tone. "You may not know this, seeing as you're awfully young, but over the centuries normies and monsters have experienced periods of friendship, periods of fear, and periods of peaceful coexistence. So the fact that we find ourselves once again in a period of fear is hardly surprising."

"Yeah, but . . ." Venus started to refute Scariff Fred's explanation when she noticed Miss Sue Nami discreetly motioning for her to stop.

As the school's Deputy of Disaster, Miss Sue Nami was Headmistress Bloodgood's second in

command. But, more important to Venus, she had long maintained her own doubts about Miss Flapper.

"But what?" Scariff Fred pressed Venus to finish her thought.

"But nothing. You're absolutely right: The normies are obviously behind this," Venus replied unconvincingly.

"Thank you, ghoul," Scariff Fred said with visible delight, and then turned to the superintendent. "Would you care to add anything, Petra?"

After offering the scariff an affirmative nod, Petra turned toward the crowd. "As the Skultastic Superintendent of Salem, I have named Miss Sue Nami acting headmistress of Monster High so that the students may maintain as normal of a routine as possible. This, of course, means that both Pic-

54

ture Day and Crack and Shield Day will occur as scheduled in a few weeks' time. And please remember, helmets are mandatory for all Crack and Shield participants, including hardheaded gargoyles."

"Wow, even the superintendent knows that gargoyles are hardheaded," Venus muttered to Rochelle.

"Superintendent Petra was referring to our stone composition, not our character."

"If you say so . . ."

CHAPTER
four

as the crowd began to disperse, Rochelle felt a drop of water land on her shoulder. But before she could even turn to look, another one fell, and then another and another. Standing directly behind the petite gray gargoyle was the perpetually waterlogged Miss Sue Nami. Bulky, brash, and decidedly unfeminine, she routinely stood with her legs wide apart and her hands perched on her hips.

"Non-adult entities, I need to see you," Miss

Sue Nami barked as she looked suspiciously around the corridor.

"But you're looking right at us? Although it is possible that water has clouded your vision," Rochelle replied sincerely. "But you needn't worry; I'm sure Cy knows a very good optometrist."

"I do," Cy piped up softly.

"Non-adult entity, I do not need an optometrist, I need to speak with you."

"But, Madame Sue Nami, you *are* speaking with us," the highly literal gargoyle replied.

"Rochelle, I've got this," Venus said, stepping in front of Miss Sue Nami seconds before she broke into her now infamous shake.

Much like a dog after a bath, she shook from her head to her toes, sending water flying every which way.

58

"Nice, real nice," Venus moaned sarcastically as she wiped her face. "Now, what can we do for you, Miss Sue Nami?"

The perennially damp dame motioned for the foursome to follow her to the corner a few feet away. Once huddled together, Miss Sue Nami shocked everyone by speaking in a whisper. It was a most surprising turn of events for a woman who had only ever spoken at one level: uncomfortably loud.

"I spent three years living among the normies, and in that time I learned a lot about them. For example: They take Halloween very seriously; they hold baseball in high regard even though it's slower than a zombie running a marathon; hot dogs are not in fact made from dogs; but most important, they solve their problems with

59

lawsuits, not kidnappings. So while everyone else buys into this normie nonsense, I want you lot to keep your eyes and ears open. And just to be clear, I said keep your eyes and ears open, not your mouths. In other words, don't go yapping about this to anyone," Miss Sue Nami muttered, and then stomped off, leaving a trail of puddles behind her.

"She really ought to hire a troll to walk after her with a mop. Puddles can be very dangerous. As a matter of fact, they are responsible for seventy-three percent of all slips," Rochelle recalled as she surveyed the many wet spots on the floor.

However, before Cy, Robecca, or Venus could even comment, a deep and regal voice cut through the corridor. The timbre, tone, and general manner of speaking instantly set the man apart, as did his

exquisite gold-and-turquoise gauze suit. But then again, he was royalty.

"Scariff? Superintendent? May I present myself? His Royal Highness Ramses de Nile," the man imperiously introduced himself. "You may bow."

"Now we know where Cleo gets her *unique* personality from," Venus said, stifling a laugh.

"Someone sure thinks he's the cat's pajamas," Robecca remarked as she watched Mr. De Nile flick an imaginary piece of lint from his impeccably tailored gauze coat.

"Mr. De Nile," the scariff responded stiffly, while grudgingly nodding his head. "What may we do for you?"

"My daughter Cleo is a princess, second in line to the scaraoh throne. And normies, as I am

sure you know, have a long and well-documented obsession with the monarchy," Ramses de Nile explained. "Therefore I believe it highly probable that my daughter will find herself the target of the next kidnapping. And as I do not wish anything to befall her, I have come here today to ask you to assign her a bodyguard."

"I'm afraid we're not in a position to dole out personal security. All of our men are busy patrolling Salem's borders," Scariff Fred responded sternly.

"Excuse me, but I couldn't help overhearing," a werecat man interrupted. "I am Tab Bee, the newly appointed guardian of Toralei Stripe, one of Monster High's most exceptional ghouls—"

"Only in her own mind," Venus muttered under her breath.

"So I must agree with His Royal Highness Mr.

De Nile. High-profile students need, dare I say, demand, extra security."

"Thank you, Mr. Bee," Mr. De Nile responded, clearly pleased that Tab had used the moniker His Royal Highness when speaking about him.

"I'm sorry, gentlemen, but it's not going to happen. Now if you'll excuse us," Scariff Fred said as he and Superintendent Petra started off down the purple-floored corridor.

"This isn't right! Children such as ours deserve protection," Cleo's father roared, stomping one of his ornate gold boots against the floor.

"As both of your ghouls are savvy, smart, and sophisticated," a silky voice hissed from behind the two men, "they would be quite the force to be reckoned with if they traveled in unison. There's strength in numbers, you know."

"What's Miss Flapper up to now?" Venus asked the others, suspiciously eyeing the petite European dragon.

Dressed in a floor-length lavender gown with silver buttons, Miss Flapper looked as spooktacular as ever. Her long bloodred hair, crisp green eyes, and delicate white wings instantly mesmerized both Ramses de Nile and Tab Bee.

"There's a calculated reason behind everything she does," Rochelle answered. "So now we just need to figure out what it is. . . ."

"Let's start by checking out what's on those papers," Venus said.

"What papers?" Cy asked.

"We stumbled across a stash of hidden papers in the

attic, but we didn't have time to read them, so I took pictures with my iCoffin," Venus said as Robecca jumped in front of the green-faced ghoul.

"And you waited until now to tell us? I thought we were the Three Monsketeers!" Robecca boiled over as she flung her arms in the air with exasperation.

"What about me?" Cy asked quietly.

"Sorry, Cy! I meant the Four Monsketeers!" Robecca blustered as she eyed Rochelle and Venus harshly.

"No need to blow a gasket, Becs. We were going to tell you. The scariff and superintendent just momentarily sidelined us."

Around nine thirty that morning, tucked away in the Libury between two bookshelves, Cy, Rochelle, and Robecca huddled around Venus and her iCoffin. With bated breath, the students watched as the plant ghoul pulled up her photo album. Lingering in the air, inciting tinges of hope, was the notion that these pictures could lead to the safe return of Headmistress Bloodgood.

At last the first photo popped up on the screen. However, within nanoseconds, anticipation turned to disappointment. The picture was so blurry that it looked more like a piece of abstract art than a written document.

"Talk about a flea's sneeze! What if they're all like this?" Robecca worried aloud.

"Then we'll be exactly where we are right

66

now—square one," Venus said as she pulled up the next photo, which was also blurred beyond recognition.

"When taking a photo with a flash it is imperative that the photographer keep his or her hand perfectly still."

"Rochelle, are all gargoyles such know-it-alls?" Venus asked lightheartedly, suppressing a grin.

"*Boo-la-la*, Venus, I do not mean to be a know-it-all! It's just that as your ghoulfriend, I wish to be as helpful as possible," Rochelle explained sincerely.

"I know and I appreciate it," the plant ghoul replied. "And for the record, I hold know-it-alls in very high regard."

Venus then flipped to the next photo, but before she was even able to register what

she saw, Robecca crashed to the floor. The sound of copper knocking against the tiles resulted in a thunderous cacophony of sounds. Momentarily overwhelmed, Rochelle and Venus froze. Luckily, Cy was quick to react, instantly bending down to check on his copper-plated friend.

"Are you okay?" the one-eyed boy asked with genuine concern.

"Ugh, not zhem again," a familiar voice droned.

Sleeping on the bottom two shelves of a nearby bookcase were the gypsy vampire twins, Rose and Blanche Van Sangre.

"Rose, vhy must these ghoulz alvays vake us from our naps?" Blanche said before releasing a long sigh.

"You ghouls are seriously selfish! Aren't you

68

even going to ask if our friend is okay?" Venus shot back.

"Come on, Blanche, let'z go to zheir room and finish our nap," Rose said as she and her sister crawled out from the shelves.

"For the last time, the school has given you your own room! So *s'il ghoul plaît*, use it!" Rochelle cried as the two pale-faced ghouls, dressed in identical velvet capes, sauntered off.

"Are you okay? Did your boiler run out of water?" Venus asked as she and Rochelle crowded around Robecca.

"It's the photo . . . I saw his name . . ." Robecca muttered as two pumpkin heads skipped through the Libury singing, their jack-o'-lanterns bobbing wildly atop their puny little bodies.

"*It's been eight hours, thirteen minutes, and*

seven seconds since Headmistress Bloodgood disappeared! We are not happy, for it's worse than we could have feared! Why, normies, why? Please stop all this before we cry!"

"I don't understand. Whose name did you see?" Rochelle asked Robecca as Venus pressed her hand against the copper ghoul's forehead.

"I think she's running a fever," Venus said as she compared Robecca's temperature to her own.

"Robecca's father crafted her out of a steam engine; her temperature levels are completely different from ours," Rochelle corrected Venus before turning back to Robecca. "You must tell us what happened. Whose name caused you to faint so suddenly?"

"My father's name is Hexiciah Steam, and it's on that paper."

CHAPTER five

t he sole legible photo taken in the attic was an untitled document with a list of names on it: Cleo's father, Mr. De Nile; Ghoulia's mother, Mrs. Yelps; Clawdeen's parents, Mr. and Mrs. Wolf; Monster High's headmistress, Ms. Bloodgood; Deuce Gorgon's mom, Mrs. Gorgon; Robecca's father, Mr. Steam; and Draculaura's father, Dracula. However, only two names were marked up: Mr. Steam and Ms. Bloodgood.

"The two names that are circled also happen

to be the two people who are missing," Rochelle thought aloud.

"Yes, but my father has been missing for over a hundred years. . . ." Robecca trailed off as she remembered the last time she saw him.

In the weeks leading up to his disappearance, Hexiciah had been keeping odd hours, often leaving the house in the middle of the night without explanation. Robecca assumed it had something to do with his research, extending normie life spans through the use of mechanical parts. But, alas, before she had the chance to ask him, he vanished into thin air. And though Robecca hadn't a single bit of proof, she firmly believed that her normie father was somehow still alive.

After getting Robecca to her feet, everyone decided it best that she head straight back to the

Chamber of Gore and Lore for some much-needed rest. However, just before they started up the creaky pink staircase to the dormitory, a familiar Mosstrailian accent captured their attention.

"Hey, mates! Where are you swimming off to? We've got a Frightingales meeting, or haven't you heard?" Lagoona Blue, dressed in pink board shorts and a white tank top, informed Robecca, Rochelle, and Venus.

"A meeting?" Rochelle repeated. "But I don't have anything on my calendar."

"It's an emergency meeting. In light of everything that has happened, Draculaura and Frankie think it's important we get together," Lagoona explained as she flipped her long, curly blond hair over her shoulder.

"In that case"—Venus turned toward Robecca

75

and Rochelle—"we better head over to the Arts and Bats room."

The Arts and Bats room, located off the main corridor, was looking even messier than usual. Ribbons, half-used tubes of paints, scissors, colored paper, glitter, and countless other items were strewn about the room. Hanging just above the doorway was a cluster of bats, which dropped bits of food atop Draculaura's and Frankie Stein's heads as they greeted members. And as usual the copresidents of the school's most exclusive all-ghouls club were clothed impeccably—Frankie in plaid capri pants and a matching sweater-vest, and Draculaura in a pink-and-black babydoll dress.

"Welcome, ghouls," Frankie said somberly as Draculaura nodded hello.

"Deary me! Fainting is an awfully tiring affair,"

Robecca remarked after taking a seat next to Rochelle and Venus. "Not that I should complain, since you two haven't slept at all, which means it's only a matter of time before Venus starts snapping worse than Chewy."

"What's that supposed to mean?" Venus asked indignantly.

"Do not get upset with Robecca. After all, it has been scientifically proven that plants become unpleasant and grumpy without adequate sleep or sunshine," Rochelle explained in her normal matter-of-fact manner.

"You know what? You might be right. I think this lack of sleep is getting to me. I think it's even causing me to hallucinate. . . ." Venus trailed off while staring dumbfounded at the door.

And Venus was hardly alone. The whole room

was staring at the door, utterly shocked by what stood before them.

"*Quelle surprise*," Rochelle said slowly as Robecca turned to see what all the commotion was about.

"Watch your claws; this is a hundred percent silk gauze, in case you didn't know," mocha-colored mummy Cleo de Nile snapped at Toralei Stripe as the two walked into the room with their arms linked together.

"No problem. But would you mind putting on some more perfume? Decomposition is seriously stinky," the orange-maned werecat shot back venomously while waving her free hand in front of her nose.

"For the last time, you lowly alley cat, I am not *deco*mposing. Just posing. And do you know why?

Because all the world's my stage," Cleo said as she flipped back her long black and brown locks of hair.

"Big deal, mummy. All the world's my catwalk," Toralei countered.

"Toralei? Cleo?" Draculaura interrupted. "Why are you ghouls holding hands?"

"Eww! We're not holding hands. We're merely allowing our arms to touch for security reasons," Toralei explained defensively.

"And for the record, I am *so* not enjoying it," Cleo announced loudly to the room.

"Security reasons?" Frankie questioned Toralei.

"Yeah, apparently her father and my guardian think we're less likely to be kidnapped if we're together," Toralei expounded, and then deftly applied lip gloss with her free hand.

"But why would the normies want to kidnap you two? Or any student, for that matter?" Frankie asked sensibly.

"Um, hello? I'm royalty," Cleo said as though it were the most obvious answer.

"And I'm the pride of the litter," Toralei purred proudly.

"Okaaaay, if you two say so," Frankie responded with an awkward smile. "Why don't you ghouls take a seat so that we can start?"

After sashaying around the room no less than three times, the two divas finally sat down. However, once seated, the two engaged in a tug-of-war with their arms. When it came to getting along, these ghouls simply hadn't a clue what they were doing.

"Ghouls, I would like to thank you all for

coming on such short notice," Draculaura addressed the room. "In light of last night's news regarding Headmistress Bloodgood, we're suspending our community service program, Project Scare and Care, until further notice."

"And while we agree with Superintendent Petra that it's important to continue with normal everyday life, we also think it's important to honor Headmistress Bloodgood in her absence," Frankie said with both her blue eye and her green eye glistening with tears.

"Clawdeen, would you please come up here?" Draculaura asked the silky-haired werewolf, who then promptly strutted to the front of the classroom.

After lowering her head and taking a deep

breath, Clawdeen looked up at the room full of ghouls.

"When I first heard about Headmistress Blood-good, I literally howled until my fangs hurt. And not just because she's our headmistress, but because she's our friend. She believes in us; she supports our talents. I mean, if it wasn't for her, I wouldn't even have applied for the Moanatella Ghostier Fashion Fellowship. Which, by the way, led to my first fashion show in Scaris! Just in case any of you missed Spectra's blog post about it," Clawdeen said before pursing her well-lacquered lips. "Anyway, I have decided to use some of my funds from the fellowship to create these shirts. . . ."

Clawdeen then held up a well-tailored T-shirt covered in studs and rhinestones with "Got

Bloodgood?" scrawled across the front.

"I should be done with the first batch of shirts later this week," Clawdeen announced as she folded up her creation. "And even though I truly believe that Headmistress Bloodgood will be back by Picture Day, if for some reason she's not, I say we wear these shirts so that when she does return she'll be able to see how much we missed her."

As soon as the meeting ended, Robecca, Rochelle, and Venus darted down the hall and up the staircase to their room in the dormitory. Not only were they exhausted and in need of a nap but also wished to talk without worrying about eavesdroppers.

"The longer Headmistress Bloodgood is gone, the further Miss Flapper and Wydowna will get

83

with their plan—whatever it is," Venus said to Rochelle and Robecca as she climbed onto her bed and dropped her head onto the pillow.

"Jeepers! We need to do something, and fast," Robecca said as small puffs of steam exited her nose and washed over her face.

"I encourage ghouls to carry *un mouchoir*, or a handkerchief," Rochelle said as she pulled one from her pocket. "Would you care to use mine?"

Robecca nodded, and then began dabbing her face, much to her friend's delight. Seeing her own preparedness at work always left Rochelle with a feeling of satisfaction.

"In regard to uncovering Miss Flapper and Wydowna's plan, I think it would be wise to start with the list. It must mean something. After all, why else would Wydowna hide it beneath a

floorboard?" Rochelle asked.

"When you say start with the list, what exactly do you mean?" Venus inquired as her eyes fluttered with fatigue.

"I think we should speak to the monsters on the list and find out what they know, if anything," Rochelle explained.

"I've always been rather curious about our classmates' parents," Robecca mumbled.

"Well, you won't be for much longer. You're about to meet them," Venus replied as she turned over onto her side and closed her eyes.

CHAPTER Six

much like a werewolf without a brush or a gorgon without sunglasses, life at Monster High just didn't feel right. A somber yet anxious air coursed through the halls, infecting all who came into contact with it. Students' steps were heavier and smiles far more infrequent. Classes carried on as usual, yet even the teachers appeared distracted. For as much as Superintendent Petra wanted life to continue normally, it simply wasn't that easy. An integral part of Monster High—Headmistress

Bloodgood—was missing and at such an uncertain time. With the purported normie plan to wall off Salem, nearly every monster on campus was feeling rather unsure.

Over a week had passed since Headmistress Bloodgood disappeared, and sensing the need for an influx of joy, Miss Sue Nami arranged for a pep rally. And so as the last bell of the day rang, waking many a slumbering bat in the hall, students made their way toward the gym. Fresh from Physical Deaducation with Coach Igor, Rochelle and Venus looked around the bustling corridor for sight or sound of Robecca.

"I know it's silly, but I worry about Robecca arriving places on time. Without a functioning internal clock, it feels like a shot in the dark that she'll actually make it in time to see the Fear

Squad perform," Rochelle explained to Venus as Cleo and Toralei approached.

"Move it, royalty coming through," Cleo announced as she and Toralei, whose arms were linked together, knocked against zombies, werewolves, and such.

"Celebutante here, move aside," Toralei added.

"Ugh! I still cannot believe I have to hang out with you. This is like the Queen of Fangland hanging out with a Goredashian," Cleo moaned before releasing a long and labored sigh.

"I don't know how Deuce puts up with you— you're such a gauze head!"

"I will never get used to seeing those two together," Venus commented, and then turned to Rochelle. "Don't worry about Robecca. It's not the end of the world if she misses the Fear

89

Squad performance. To be honest, the only reason I'm going is because we need to get invited to Ghoulia's, Clawdeen's, Draculaura's, Cleo's, and Deuce's houses, and they're all going to be there."

"I have never been very good at getting myself invited to friends' houses. I think it has something to do with the safety inspection I ask to perform upon arriving," Rochelle muttered as she spotted Miss Flapper talking to Jinafire Long and Skelita Calaveras in the hall. "*Boo-la-la*, I see she is still wielding her influence or whatever it is over those two. . . ."

"I think they're just impressed by her beauty and couture clothes. If it was another Whisper spell, it would have spread to others by now," Venus speculated as she eyed the European

dragon up and down. "I may not like her, but she sure does dress well. Just look at that delicate shrug."

"Yes, I was just noticing that. It looks awfully similar to the lacelike fabric we saw in the attic. I suspect the spider ghoul is not just her partner in crime but her couturier," Rochelle said as she narrowed her eyes and shook her head.

"You know what's funny? You sound more annoyed about the couturier part than the crime part!" Venus joked as she raised her green eyebrows at her friend.

"*Mais non*," Rochelle protested as the two entered the gym.

The shiny wooden Casketball court was surrounded by green bleachers and purple windows covered in spindly bars.

As nearly the entire school was present, Rochelle and Venus had to weather quite a crowd of creatures just to find a couple of free seats. Squeezed between a zombie and a werewolf, the ghouls felt pangs of sadness upon noting the many gloomy expressions on the faces in the crowd.

"*Quelle surprise!*" Rochelle gushed as she pointed across the court to the other set of bleachers.

"Is that Becs sitting next to Deuce?" Venus said as she narrowed her eyes to get a better look.

"Yes, it most definitely is. . . ."

"Maybe Becs is learning to keep track of time," Venus suggested, prompting Rochelle to shake her head incredulously. "Or . . . Deuce ran into her in the hall and walked her over here."

Just then the Fear Squad—Frankie, Draculaura,

92

Clawdeen, and Cleo—walked onto the court. However, as Cleo was currently "attached" to Toralei, the werecat had no choice but to join the squad for the pep rally. It was a rather tense addition as Toralei had previously grumbled at the fearleaders for "jumping around and annoying" her.

"I think convincing Cleo to have us over to her house is going to prove *très* difficult," Rochelle whispered to Venus as the Fear Squad lined up to start their performance.

"More difficult than cheering while holding another ghoul's arm?" Venus remarked as she watched Cleo and Toralei awkwardly attempt to start the routine.

"Listen up, ghouls and boys, we're here to get you smiling!" Frankie called into her bullhorn as

the other fearleaders started clapping. Or more precisely, all but Cleo and Toralei started clapping. The tempestuous twosome was incapable of getting in sync.

"*Give me an S, an M, an I, an L, an E! SMILE! It's time to turn up the dial and make all you monsters smile!*" the fearleaders cheered as they started kicking their legs in the air.

"Ouch!" Cleo grunted. "Stop kicking me!"

"You stop! Werecat fur should never be touched by shoes! Especially ugly shoes!"

"How dare you call my shoes ugly?! I'll have you know that Alexander McScream designed these especially for me!" Cleo responded while shaking her head at the werecat.

Cleo and Toralei stood in the middle of the court arguing passionately with each other, seemingly

not bothered by the fact that the squad was in the middle of a routine. Annoyed and wishing to contain the distraction, Frankie motioned for the rest of the team to surround the duo and continue cheering.

"*We can't waste another day, just because the headmistress is away! We must make her proud, by living out loud!*" the fearleaders chanted while flailing their arms and legs about in perfect unison.

It was at this point that a pod of pumpkin heads bounced onto the court. The group of eight large-headed creatures then started singing a cappella.

"*The fearleaders are here, to fill you with cheer! So turn your frown upside down, and Bloodgood will soon be back 'round!*"

At this point all the fearleaders, except Cleo and Toralei, began chanting "Smile!"

95

Nearby, a couple of trolls began scanning the crowd for somber faces. Upon seeing one, the grimy little monsters bellowed, "Smile now! It's the rules! The fearleaders say 'Smile!' Ignore fearleaders, make trolls mad, then you be sorry!"

"Trolls, there's no need to threaten the non-adult entities," Miss Sue Nami called from the bleachers. "Not yet anyway."

Following the pep rally, students and teachers leisurely mingled on the Casketball court. And though the problems facing Monster High and the town of Salem remained, there was no denying that the pep rally had lifted everyone's spirits.

"Good news, ghouls! I got us an invite to Deuce's house tomorrow after school," Robecca declared happily as she ran across the Casketball court to Rochelle and Venus.

Thrilled by her accomplishment, Robecca flicked the switch on her jet-pack boots and performed a quick backflip. It was, like all of her aerial maneuvers, very impressive.

"Robecca! You're amazing! Honestly, I'm so impressed that you even remembered to ask him," Rochelle declared as she kissed the copper-plated ghoul on the cheek.

"But I didn't. It wasn't until he asked me over that I remembered the plan. You see, I've been so preoccupied thinking about my father that I haven't even thought about the list. . . ."

"Then how did you get an invite?" Venus wondered aloud.

"Deuce asked me if I could come over and steam the snakes on his Mohawk," Robecca explained.

"But why would he want you to do that?" Venus continued.

"Snake skin can get super dry and scaly," Robecca explained.

"Ah, I understand now. He wants to give them a spa treatment," Rochelle said while nodding her head. "Which is an activity better done in the privacy of one's own home than at school."

"Well, I guess that just leaves Cleo, Clawdeen, Ghoulia, and Draculaura," Venus said as she looked over at a cluster of ghouls standing on the court. "Maybe we should try Frankie too."

98

"But her parents weren't on the list," Robecca pointed out.

"That doesn't mean they don't know something about it," countered Venus.

"Okay, why don't Robecca and I handle Clawdeen, Frankie, Ghoulia, and Draculaura, and you take Cleo?" suggested Rochelle.

"No way!" Venus scoffed.

"That actually sounds like a pretty swell idea, seeing as you're probably going to have to use your pollens of persuasion to get Cleo to invite us over," Rochelle added.

"Fine," Venus agreed, and then slowly made her way toward Cleo and Toralei.

Standing with their arms linked and their backs touching, the ghouls were clearly doing their best to avoid interacting with each other.

99

"Hey, Cleo," Venus said trepidatiously as she approached the always stylish, gauze-clad ghoul.

"Hello," Cleo drawled in her usual terse manner.

"I guess now you know what it's like to be a Siamese twin," Venus joked while nervously fiddling with her vines.

"More like a cry-amese twin, since being so close to a werecat makes me want to cry," Cleo muttered under her breath. "Honestly, I wouldn't be surprised if I were allergic to her."

"I'm beginning to think getting taken by the normies a better alternative to staying with a spoiled ghoul like you! Oh, and by spoiled, I mean rotten, foul, putrid—"

"Someone's been studying her SAT vocabulary

words," Venus interrupted Toralei in an effort to lighten the tone.

"What is it exactly that you're doing here?" Cleo asked Venus.

"In the gym? There was a pep rally, remember?"

"I meant in front of me," Cleo snapped.

"I wanted to ask if I could come over to your tomb tomorrow after school," Venus uttered clumsily.

"You want to come to my tomb? I don't think so. . . ."

"It's just that you're the most stylish ghoul on campus, perhaps even in the Boo World, and it would be such an honor to see your closet," Venus carried on theatrically.

"Stylish? Compared to me she's nothing more than a flea," Toralei spouted off.

"Um, Toralei, this is a two-person conversation, so if you could quiet down I would really appreciate it," Venus said before turning back to Cleo. "I could even help you with your garden, if you like. After all, mummies aren't known for their green thumbs."

"Green really suits me. But then again, all colors do," Cleo responded confidently.

"So what do you say? Can I come by after school with Robecca and Rochelle?"

"Sorry, but my aunty Neferia is visiting from the Old World and she doesn't hold plant monsters, steam creations, or gargoyles in high regard. She's super strict about only socializing with scaraohs, vampires, and aristocratic ghosts," Cleo explained before narrowing her eyes at Venus. "Plus, I suspect you have an ulterior motive."

"An ulterior motive? Me? Never!" Venus fibbed unconvincingly.

"I think you want to come over so you can look for things to recycle," Cleo said suspiciously.

"I wish someone would recycle this whole conversation," Toralei interjected with a huff.

"Recycling is nothing to joke about. Unless, of course, you find destroying the planet funny," Venus blustered, her face now visibly red.

"This weed is crazy obsessed with garbage," Toralei remarked rudely.

"On that we can agree," Cleo responded as Venus continued to smart over their callous attitude toward the environment.

"You think I'm crazy? You want to know what's crazy? Tossing chemicals into the ocean! Stuffing trash into mountains! That's crazy!" Venus roared

as a powerful rush of pollens pumped through her vines.

"ACHOO!" Venus sounded, releasing a pollen-filled sneeze.

However, just as the pollen made its way toward Cleo, Toralei tugged at her arm, inadvertently pulling her out of the line of fire. Small orange particles then splashed upon a blue-haired, floppy-bodied, button-eyed boy standing close by.

"Hoodude!" Venus screamed as the life-size voodoo doll experienced a light smattering of pollen.

"Yes, my wonderful Venus?" Hoodude responded adoringly.

"Oh no," Venus groaned before releasing a long, labored sigh.

"What's the matter, my most precious friend?"

Hoodude asked, placing his soft fabric-covered hand on Venus's shoulder.

"I'm not your most precious friend. Remember Frankie Stein? You know the ghoul that you're in love with? The one who created you?" Venus replied.

"The only ghoul I ever wish to lay my button eyes upon again is you, the wondrous Venus McFlytrap. The sole plant in the garden of my heart." Hoodude waxed poetic.

"Eww, the doll likes the plant," Toralei muttered meanly.

"Can it, cat lady," Venus shot back aggressively as she looked over at Robecca and Rochelle successfully chatting away with Clawdeen, Frankie, Ghoulia, and Draculaura.

Venus sighed. The pollen approach was a bust.

Securing invitations to Clawdeen's, Ghoulia's, Frankie's, and Draculaura's houses proved surprisingly simple. Robecca and Rochelle merely told the ghouls that they wanted to see the inside of an average Salem home. With the supposed normie invasion looming on the horizon, Monster High's students were more grateful than usual for their everyday lives. Specifically, for their bedrooms, uniquely decorated to reflect their taste; for the shops at the Maul; for the Die-ner; for the Coffin Bean; and most important, for the ability to move across borders without normie permission. And so when Robecca and Rochelle asked to

visit Draculaura's, Ghoulia's, Clawdeen's, and Frankie's homes, the ghouls happily acquiesced.

After securing invitations, Robecca, Rochelle, and Venus decided to try their luck in the attic again. For if by any chance Wydowna were out, they would be able to peruse the other papers and possibly garner additional information. And so after waiting for night to come and the bats to rumble, the trio threw back their covers, grabbed their robes, and tiptoed out of the Chamber of Gore and Lore.

"Personally, I have always held true that when engaging in secret missions one ought to wear appropriate clothing. And I hardly think pajamas and dressing gowns are appropriate. After all, running in a robe is no easy task," Rochelle whispered as the trio started up the stairs to the attic.

"Until things go totally haywire, there will be absolutely no running in tonight's mission," Venus replied as her slippered feet continued up the stone steps.

"Ouch!" Robecca blurted out loudly.

"What is it?" Venus asked with concern.

"Chewy just bit my finger!" Robecca whined.

"This is exactly why I said we should leave the pets in our room. They are nothing but a distraction," Rochelle declared firmly.

"How can you even say that? Haven't you noticed how depressed they've been?" Robecca said while shaking her head dramatically.

"Roux is never depressed," Rochelle quickly corrected her friend.

"Okay, fine, but Chewy and Penny have most definitely been depressed. So you can hardly blame me for thinking a little adventure might cheer them up."

"Becs, is that really why you insisted on bringing them?" Venus asked skeptically.

"Well, I may have also thought that Chewy could distract Wydowna's pet fly if need be," Robecca explained quietly.

"Let's just hope he doesn't eat her. After all, Chewy does have a taste for flies . . . and jewelry and metal and paper." Venus quieted down as they once again came upon the entryway to the attic adorned in elegantly woven webs.

"Someone needs to discreetly look inside and

109

see if Wydowna's there," Venus said, looking directly at Rochelle.

"*Boo-la-la! Pourquoi moi?* Why me?"

"You have sharp claws to cut through the webbing and you don't steam when you get nervous," Robecca explained.

"*Zut!*" Rochelle said as she began to carefully slice through the webs.

Rochelle then crawled through the sheaths, only to quickly retreat back into the stairwell seconds later.

"Wydowna and her fly friend are sleeping in the hammock, but . . ."

"But what?" Robecca pressed Rochelle eagerly.

"There was the most beautiful jacket I have ever seen just lying on the floor. She clearly does

110

not realize how *fangtastique* her creations are. The details—"

"Not to be a fashion-pessimista, but it's after midnight, so what do you say we save the dramatic retelling of her clothes until tomorrow?" Venus said as she started back down the stairs with Chewy in hand.

A couple days later, Robecca, Rochelle, and Venus found themselves seated at the counter in the Stein family kitchen. The stainless-steel room was filled with an array of modern appliances, oddly colored vials, and a professional sewing machine.

Yet even with all these contraptions the kitchen somehow still managed to feel both warm and familial.

"Frankie tells me the Creepateria food can get a little repetitive," Mrs. Stein said as she placed a plate of BLTs—beast, lettuce, and tomato—on the counter.

"Mother, I never said repetitive. I said bland," Frankie exclaimed, and then turned toward the trio. "It's like they've never even heard of pepper! And pepper is so voltage!"

"I love pepper. Pepper really is the best. Absolutely swell. Say, Frankie, would you care to see my peppercorn collection? I just so happen to have it with me in my school bag," Robecca babbled clumsily as she stood up.

"Wait, you have a peppercorn collection?"

Frankie asked Robecca. "And you carry it around with you?"

"Yes, I do," Robecca fibbed poorly. "So what do you say? Do you want to see my peppercorn collection or not?"

"I thought we told her to be subtle," Venus muttered discreetly to Rochelle.

"Clearly *subtle* is a subjective concept," Rochelle whispered back to Venus. "As are credible fibs . . . a peppercorn collection? What was she thinking?"

"You want me to come with you right now? But we're about to eat," Frankie explained to Robecca.

"Oh, go on, dear. It sounds like tons of fun," Mrs. Stein said, winking at her mint-green daughter playfully.

113

"All right," Frankie agreed reluctantly, and then stood and followed Robecca out of the room.

Once alone with Frankie's mother, Rochelle promptly took out Venus's iCoffin, pulled up the picture of the list, and showed it to Mrs. Stein.

"*Pardonnez-moi*, Madame Stein. Do you have any idea what this list might mean? Why Headmistress Bloodgood's and Hexiciah Steam's names are circled?" Rochelle questioned the woman directly.

"Talk about dying on the vine; do *any* of my friends know how to be subtle?" Venus moaned to herself as a startled Mrs. Stein took the iCoffin from Rochelle.

After staring at the photographed document for a few seconds, Mrs. Stein turned a pasty shade of white, or more precisely an extremely pale shade

of green. Then, as Rochelle and Venus exchanged curious glances, Mrs. Stein quickly dabbed the sweat off her upper lip and tried her best to regain her composure.

"I'm sorry, ghouls, but I haven't a clue what this list might be," Mrs. Stein said as she pulled off her apron and placed it on the counter. "Now then, I'm so sorry to run off, but I promised to help Mr. Stein in his laboratory this afternoon, so I really must be going."

"But . . ." Venus started to say as Mrs. Stein darted out of the room.

Nearly identical scenes unfolded at Ghoulia's, Draculaura's, and Clawdeen's houses with their

parents denying any knowledge of the list. Yet so markedly similar were the reactions that Robecca, Rochelle, and Venus knew they had to be onto something.

"Now remember, Becs, let Rochelle do the talking. I think we can all agree that acting is not your strong suit," Venus lectured as they mounted the steps to Deuce's house.

"It's funny how much I used to swoon at the mere mention of Deuce. And now I consider him no more than a friend. It's quite surprising. For, when one is in the throes of a crush, it seems utterly impossible that the emotions might change or wane," Rochelle finished as she rang the doorbell.

Deuce's mother, Mrs. Gorgon, answered the door in a long green caftan and oversize Croako

116

Chanel sunglasses. Not that anyone noticed, since they were all rather taken aback by her wild head of orange, yellow, and red snakes. Much like a sunset, the snakes' skins seemed to bleed into one another as they slithered animatedly around her head.

"Hello, young ghouls, may I help you?" Mrs. Gorgon asked in a kind yet formal manner.

"*Boo-jour*, Mrs. Gorgon, we're Deuce's friends Robecca, Rochelle, and Venus."

"Ah yes, of course, I've heard much about you three. Unfortunately, Deuce isn't home yet, but you're welcome to come in and wait," she said with a smile, stepping back and motioning for the trio to enter. "And please call me Medusa."

Robecca, Rochelle, and Venus were led into a Goreroccan-style living room with arched

windows and sumptuous couches covered in red snakeskin.

"Please have a seat," Medusa said warmly to the ghouls. "May I offer you some English Dreadfast tea?"

"Oh, that would be swell! I can even boil the water if you'd like," Robecca offered sweetly.

"That's very kind of you, but you needn't trouble yourself," Medusa said as a snake flapped about on her neck. "Snakes can be so unruly," she said as she swatted at it. "They're a bit like trolls; they never listen to anyone."

And with that Mrs. Gorgon sashayed out of the living room.

"She's *trés* sophisticated, *n'est-ce pas*?" Rochelle said to Venus and Robecca.

"Totally," Venus said as she pulled up the

photograph of the list on her iCoffin.

"Heavens to *Bat*sy!" Robecca said with a gulp. "Do you think she made that statue herself?"

Standing next to the fireplace was an intricate and lifelike stone statue of a bat.

"It looks seriously realistic," Venus commented as she stood to get a closer look.

"Ah, I see you've spotted last week's little mishap," Medusa said as she entered carrying a tray of tea.

"It's very becoming to the fireplace." Rochelle inelegantly attempted to cover up their interest in the statue.

"Sometimes I forget to put my sunglasses on and then things like this happen. But not to worry, he'll be back to normal in a week or two," Medusa said as she began to pour Robecca's tea. "Ghouls,

I'm sorry to say that Deuce just texted, and he's been delayed by Cleo. You know mummies, they're easy to get wrapped up in."

"Oh, we understand," Venus said. "But since we're here, could we ask you a question?"

"Of course," she replied as she attempted to calm her snakes with another pat of the hand.

Venus then walked over and placed the iCoffin on the table in front of Mrs. Gorgon, who shortly thereafter inspected the picture.

"Hmmm. How strange that Ramses's name is missing," Deuce's mom muttered almost inaudibly to herself.

"*Pardonnez-moi*? What was that you said?" Rochelle asked inquisitively, tapping her nails atop the metal coffee table.

"Nothing. I said nothing. Now, ghouls, if you'll

excuse me, I have much work to attend to," Medusa said as she rose from her seat and handed Venus back her iCoffin.

"But if we could—"

"I'm sorry, but I simply don't have time for any more questions," Medusa interrupted Venus harshly.

And with that she rushed Robecca, Rochelle, and Venus back through the house and out the door with a firm push.

CHAPTER

Seven

the pink coffin-shaped lockers that lined the halls of Monster High were covered with posters, pictures, and letters pertaining to Headmistress Bloodgood's kidnapping. It had been more than three weeks since her disappearance, and still no one had a clue where she was or how to stop the "normie wall." It was a scenario that left the halls of Monster High rife with frustration, gloominess, and fear.

As Rochelle made her way down the main corridor past the sea of Headmistress Bloodgood

123

posters, she heard a familiar voice call out her name.

"Hey, Rochelle, wait up," Deuce said as he overtook a troop of slow-moving zombies in the corridor.

"*Boo-jour*, Deuce," Rochelle offered warmly. "If this is about Trick and Treat, I told them that we wouldn't be able to start their tutoring again until after Headmistress Bloodgood was found. Although, I must say, I find their sudden interest in studying most surprising, since they hardly listened to a word I said during our lessons."

"Poor Trick and Treat. They're taking Headmistress Bloodgood's disappearance harder than a diamond."

"The Gargoyle Code of Ethics states that I must correct inaccurate information; therefore I would

like to inform you that while diamonds were once considered the hardest stone in the Boo World, that is no longer true. Scientists recently found that lonsdaleite and wurtzite boron nitrade are in fact harder," Rochelle clarified, prompting Deuce to smile.

"In that case, Trick, Treat, and the other trolls are taking Headmistress Bloodgood's disappearance harder than lonsdaleite and wurtzite boron nitrade," Deuce said with a wink. "They feel like

they let Headmistress Bloodgood down, that her disappearance is their fault."

"That is absolutely preposterous. The trolls are essentially hall monitors! Not members of the Creature Intelligence Agency," Rochelle said, before looking down at her watch. "I loathe to chat and run, but as you know, I take punctuality very seriously."

"Of course, I just wanted to say sorry I didn't get home in time to meet you ghouls yesterday—I had to referee a fight between Cleo and Toralei. They were both seething with rage. . . . It was actually kind of freaky."

"Well, they *have* been spending an inordinate amount of time together. Plus, they are both very spirited ghouls."

"Yeah, especially when they realize they're

wearing the same shirt," Deuce said as he shook his head.

"I can only imagine," Rochelle responded. "And you needn't worry about yesterday. We very much enjoyed having tea with your mother—she's so stylish and sophisticated."

"Who's stylish and sophisticated?" a voice hissed from behind Rochelle.

"*Boo-la-la*! Where did you come from?"

"You know me, Rochelle. I'm always around," Miss Flapper replied as she came up behind them and then continued gliding down the hall.

"She's very strange, *n'est-ce pas*?" Rochelle mumbled to Deuce.

"Definitely," Deuce replied. "Speaking of strange, did you say something to my mom?"

"What do you mean?" Rochelle replied as

her mouth went as dry as werewolf fur in the summer.

"When I got home she was acting sort of skittish, and then I heard her whispering on the phone."

"What was she saying?" Rochelle inquired, anxiously tapping her claws against her book bag.

"Something about some society using you, Robecca, and Venus to try and get information out of her," Deuce finished.

"Ah yes. She must have been referring to my questions about how she decorated her home. I guess she thinks we're moles for other designers," Rochelle poorly covered, all the while scratching her claws loudly against her bag.

"You are officially the worst liar in the Boo World, and I do mean worst. Seriously, I've

seen trolls lie more convincingly than you."

"*S'il ghoul plaît*, Deuce, do not tell anyone what you overheard. I can't explain right now, so you're just going to have to trust me. Do you think you can do that?"

"I think so," Deuce said with a smile.

"Wonderful," Rochelle said as she once again looked at her watch. "Now I really must be going. Mr. Mummy might worry if I'm late to Catacombing."

Rochelle waved good-bye to Deuce and turned to leave.

"Rochelle?"

"Yes?" the hardheaded ghoul responded.

"Did you forget that I'm in Catacombing class with you?"

"*Boo alors*! But of course," Rochelle said with

a smile as the two made their way toward the ornate gold elevator to the Catacombs.

So loquacious was Mr. Mummy on this particular day that Rochelle was unable to tell Venus and Robecca about her conversation with Deuce until after the period had ended. As soon as the bell rang, the granite ghoul motioned for her friends to stay behind. And when the last of the students moved out of earshot, Rochelle quickly brought Robecca and Venus up-to-date.

"What society could Medusa be referring to?" Venus asked, seated at a table in a corner of the Catacombs classroom.

The stone-walled room, located within the vast collection of underground tunnels, was surprisingly lively, as it was crammed with colorful furniture crafted out of bones, stones, and twigs.

"You don't think she meant the Society of Fangs and Fur, do you?" Robecca whispered, and then quickly looked over at Mr. Mummy to make sure he hadn't overheard.

"Becs, the Society of Fangs and Fur is a beauty salon. It's not a real society," Venus explained while shaking her head.

"Well, she certainly didn't mean the Frightingale Society," Rochelle addcd as Mr. Mummy began to eye the trio curiously.

Wrapped in crisp white gauze and wearing a tweed suit, their always-dapper teacher approached the threesome.

"Ghouls, I realize you might be disappointed that you didn't get to dig today, but believe me, my lecture was very important. And I promise tomorrow you'll be back up to your elbows in sand."

"Oh, it's not that, Mr. Mummy. We just lost track of time, which, of course, I do all the time. Ugh! Why do I keep uttering that dreadful word? I don't even like hearing the word *time*, never mind saying it! And yet I just did it again!" Robecca babbled as Venus eyed their teacher.

"Mr. Mummy, you know a great deal about both the Boo World and the Old World, don't you?" Venus inquired, her vines bristling with curiosity.

Mr. Mummy always loved a compliment, especially concerning his intelligence. And so

he lowered his head in false humility and nodded.

"Venus, I may not be a scaraoh, but I have a B.A. from King Tut's Teachers College, which is one of the finest universities in the world. Gill Baits once went there. . . ."

"You mean he's an alumnus?" Rochelle asked, looking for clarification.

"No . . . he once went there . . . for a meeting. Or actually I think he might have gotten lost and stopped for directions," Mr. Mummy clarified quietly.

"I feel like I'm always asking for directions. If only my father had thought to put a GPS system in me," Robecca muttered to herself.

"Regardless of who attended your college, you know a lot about the world," Venus again com-

plimented her teacher. "And that's why I want to ask you a question."

"Venus, gargoyles consider announcing that you are going to ask a question *très* redundant," Rochelle said, prompting her friend to smile.

"Point taken, Rochelle. Now, Mr. Mummy, have you ever heard of a society that might elicit fear in other monsters?" Venus asked.

"And she's not talking about the Frightingales, even though we all know that Cleo and Toralei have been known to elicit fear in those around them," Robecca added, shaking her head at the mere thought of the difficult duo.

"Let me think," Mr. Mummy said as he rubbed his chin. "There was the Society for Furless Werewolves, but it's been years since anyone's heard even a growl from them."

"Furless werewolves?" Rochelle repeated back to Mr. Mummy. "*C'est très* bizarre."

"The Society for Furless Werewolves was formed by a group of aestheticians hoping to make a killing in the hair removal business," Mr. Mummy explained.

"Anything else?" Venus pressed her teacher. "Maybe something a little more sinister."

Mr. Mummy paused, swallowed audibly, and then looked around nervously.

"What's the matter, Mr. Mummy?" Rochelle asked. "Are you worried someone might overhear what you have to say?"

"As a teacher, I do not like to repeat rumors or really anything that has not been proven scientifically. What's this about anyway?"

"We're doing a project in Monstory about

secret societies," Venus spouted off quickly.

"In that case, I definitely won't share this with you. Students should never reference rumors in an academic paper," Mr. Mummy said, and then turned to leave.

"Wait!" Robecca blurted out in a panic. "You don't understand. Mr. Mummy, um, we're supposed to write a made-up story inspired by real events. I suppose it's what you might call . . . historical fiction?"

"Well, in that case I guess it's okay," Mr. Mummy said before taking a seat at the table. "There have long been rumors in the Old World that there is a secret society whose members believed in a hierarchy of monsters. That some species were more important than others."

"And have you ever heard rumors about this

group in the Boo World?" Rochelle asked as she tapped her sharp claws against the top of the table.

"Not that I know of, but alas, there is much I don't know. . . ."

"Yeah, us too," Venus mumbled.

CHAPTER
eight

obecca, Rochelle, and Venus rode the elevator up from the Catacombs in silence, each mulling over what Mr. Mummy had said. The idea of a creature hierarchy was a hard concept to fathom, as they had been raised to believe that all monsters were created equal. As a matter of fact, outside of Cleo's mention of her aunt Neferia believing that some monsters were superior to others, the trio had never even heard of such a thing.

"Rochelle, smile! Miss Sue Nami says smile! Now!" Trick grunted angrily at the gargoyle as she stepped off the elevator and into the main corridor.

"*Pardonnez-moi*, Trick, but this is not a police state. I do not have to smile unless I want to," Rochelle huffed intensely.

"Miss Sue Nami says everyone must smile. No more sad!" the troll declared before waddling off down the hall.

"So now she's trying to *mully* the students into being happy?" Venus asked Robecca and Rochelle. "I don't think she understands that the longer Headmistress Bloodgood is gone, the more the students fear the threat of the wall. I mean, just this morning I heard Blanche and Rose Van Sangre talking about their plan to shave off their fangs and

pass themselves off as extremely pale normies."

"That is absolutely ridiculous," Rochelle declared loudly.

"I know, right?" Venus agreed with Rochelle.

"Actually, Venus, I was referring to your use of the term *mully*. How many times must I tell you that it is not a real word? And, *chérie*, I only say this because you are my friend and I wish you to speak correctly—" Rochelle responded before pausing abruptly. "*Regardez*, something's happened to Madame Flapper!"

Miss Flapper was leaning against Jinafire Long as she slowly made her way down the main corridor. With both Jinafire's green tail and gold arm wrapped around Miss Flapper for support, it appeared as though the teacher was too weak to walk on her own.

"Eek! Look at that poor hem!" Robecca squealed, staring at a large tear along the bottom of Miss Flapper's billowy coral dress.

"Forget the dress; look at her hair," Venus chimed in as she inspected the normally fastidiously groomed teacher's tangled locks.

"Perhaps she fell," Rochelle theorized. "Or attempted to take food from a troll? They're notoriously territorial about their ghoulash and pus pastries."

"There is an old Fanghai proverb: A successful plan of attack requires much research," Jinafire said to the visibly rattled teacher as they passed by Robecca, Rochelle, and Venus in the hall.

"Jeepers creepers, what happened?" Robecca called out to Miss Flapper and Jinafire.

"*Fūrén* Flapper was walking along the edge of

142

town when a normie saw her and then attempted to kidnap her," Jinafire explained.

"I was so scared. He tried to kidnap me just like Headmistress Bloodgood," Miss Flapper muttered softly.

"So a normie did this to Miss Flapper?" Venus pondered with genuine surprise.

"No. Luckily she was able to dart into a nearby Thornberry bush until the man retreated back across the border," Jinafire explained. "But, of course, Thornberry bushes are filled with thorns; hence her disheveled appearance."

"Scariff Fred says the man was a spy sent to gather information on us. But of course he wasn't expecting anyone to see him, which is why he tried to take me," Miss Flapper explained, furrowing her brow.

"With all due respect, Madame Flapper, are you sure the normie was trying to kidnap you and not simply have a conversation with you?" Rochelle asked directly.

"I know you're scared, and I wish with all my heart that I could allay your fears and tell you that the normie just wanted to chat . . . but I can't. . . ." Miss Flapper stated dramatically before wiping away a lone tear.

"Our teacher must rest now," Jinafire said as she continued down the hall with the tousled woman.

"What a load of garbage," Venus muttered to Robecca and Rochelle as soon as the two were out of earshot.

"News flash: Miss Flapper escapes normie abduction!" Spectra Vondergeist called out as

she came floating down the hall with her iCoffin in hand. "Check out my blog for the latest information!"

As the ghouls continued down the main corridor, they noticed a most unusual pairing passing out flyers in front of the Vampitheater—Cy and Miss Sue Nami.

"What's this about?" Robecca asked as she took a flyer from Cy.

"Non-adult entities, Operetta will be performing her new song tomorrow, 'Give Us Back Our Rockin' Headmistress, Normies.' I'm really hoping it will help boost morale," Miss Sue Nami stated matter-of-factly.

"Boost morale? The title of the song sounds like it's promoting the idea that Headmistress Bloodgood was kidnapped by the normies, and we

145

all know that's not the case," Venus confronted Monster High's acting headmistress.

"Non-adult entity, you are irritatingly right. But as I have learned, there's no point arguing something unless you have proof. So in the meantime, I'm doing my best to keep the other non-adult entities hopeful."

"But what do you have to do with Operetta's gig?" Robecca asked Cy.

"Nothing. He just happened to be walking by when I realized I needed another pair of hands," Miss Sue Nami barked. "The concert will take place tomorrow at lunchtime in the Creepateria. I expect to see all three of you ghouls there."

"The chef's preparing barbecue critters to give the concert a true Southern vibe," Cy added.

"No running in the hall!" Miss Sue Nami

hollered at a nearby werewolf, and then stomped off.

"She isn't much for good-byes, is she?" Venus commented.

"Anyone up for a snack? Hanging out with Miss Sue Nami really builds up my appetite," Cy asked the ghouls.

"Absolutely. Plus, we have a lot to fill you in on," Robecca replied.

While walking into town, the trio told Cy about what Mr. Mummy had said about the secret society, and of course about Miss Flapper's supposed kidnapping attempt by a normie.

"It's not just Monster High that's buying into the normie propaganda," Robecca said as she paused in front of the entrance to the Die-ner.

147

Displayed just to the left of the door was a large poster with the following message:

SALEM SHOPPERS:

THERE'S NO SUCH THING AS A WELL-STOCKED MAUL INSIDE OF A PRISON WALL. JOIN THE VOLUNTEER BORDER PATROL TODAY AND HELP STOP THE NORMIES!

"The situation is clearly escalating. Just look around," Cy said as he pointed out skittish, mistrustful, and frightened-looking men, women,

and children walking around downtown Salem.

"Jeez Louise, what are we going to do? We can't just stand by and let our school and our town fall to pieces!" Robecca screeched once seated with Rochelle, Venus, and Cy in a tufted pink booth inside the Die-ner.

"You must calm down, *chérie*. Grinding your gears will not help the situation," Rochelle advised Robecca.

"Maybe we should check out the Crybrary to see if there's anything in there on this society," Cy suggested after taking a sip of his Croak-a-Cola.

"The what?" Robecca asked as she pushed a long and golden Crunch Cry into her mouth.

"Don't you remember the Crybrary? Where we found the information on how to break the Whisper?" Venus reminded Robecca.

"Oh yes, of course," Robecca replied. "The secret Libury hidden behind the Absolutely Deranged Scientist Laboratory."

"I think that is a very good idea, Cy," Rochelle said as she used a fork and knife to eat a Crunch Cry.

"Well, as they say, there's no time like the present," Venus stated as she stood up from the booth.

"As who says?" Rochelle inquired seriously.

"As monsters say," Venus replied.

"Which monsters?"

"Just monsters!" Venus huffed as the group made its way to the Die-ner's door.

After walking through the test tube and Bunsen burner–filled Absolutely Deranged Scientist Laboratory, the quartet entered the utility closet at the back of the room. The small and utilitarian space contained a sink, broom stand, water main, and little else. In fact, if they hadn't already known what to look for, the Crybrary would have been virtually impossible to find.

"Who wants to do the honors?" Venus asked Cy, Robecca, and Rochelle.

"I would, if you don't mind," Rochelle said before forcefully lobbing her stone foot against the doorjamb.

Almost immediately the sound of metal grinding against metal filled the room as a thick ladder descended from the ceiling.

"I would be *très contente* to climb the ladder,

but as we all know, granite is not always kind to items such as these," Rochelle stated honestly.

"Don't worry, I've got this one," Venus said as she carefully secured her vines and then started climbing up the ladder.

Upon reaching the ceiling, the green-skinned ghoul crawled a few feet across and then lowered herself into a minuscule and highly claustrophobic room. The walls of the three-feet-by-three-feet space were lined from floor to ceiling with thick leather-bound books.

"Here's hoping this doesn't take longer than photosynthesis in the dark," Venus mumbled to herself as she began scanning the spines of the books, stopping when she came across the title *The Secrets of Secret Societies*.

Venus's eyes widened with excitement as

152

she attempted to pull the book from the shelf. Only she couldn't, because it was chained to the wall. It was, of course, the only means of stopping monsters from removing the important tomes and possibly forgetting to return them. Venus immediately started flipping through the pages, looking for any mention of an Old World society that believed in a hierarchy of monsters.

Minutes turned into an hour, and then another hour, as the green ghoul scoured the pages of the antique leather book. Annoyed and frustrated, she twice put the book down, but quickly picked it up after thinking of Headmistress Bloodgood. However, upon finishing the last page of the book, the ghoul's heart sank with disappointment. There was nothing in there even remotely similar

153

to what Mr. Mummy had described. Perhaps it really was just a rumor.

Why had she wasted hours investigating something that didn't exist? Venus wondered to herself. Visibly annoyed, she forcefully flipped the last page and prepared to slam the book shut. But at the last second she caught sight of some faint scribbling on the back flap of the book.

ASOME — The only way to keep them at bay is to educate the next generation. Teach them that all monsters are created equal.

"It's not much, but it's something," Venus muttered to herself as she pulled out her iCoffin to snap a photo of the message.

"ASOME? What an odd name for a society," Rochelle stated the following day as the trio munched on barbecue critters and waited for Operetta to arrive for her performance in the Creepateria.

"Maybe it's an Old World name?" Venus suggested.

"Or the founder's name?" Robecca pondered as everyone around them buzzed with anxiety over Miss Flapper's "near kidnapping by a normie" the day before.

"I heard the normie was so taken with her beauty that he couldn't remember what he was doing. That's how she was able to escape," Clawdeen babbled nervously to Lagoona.

"I'm not sure about that, mate," Lagoona replied. "Because I heard that Miss Flapper was

155

forced to use a Thornberry branch to defend herself."

"I heard the same thing," Frankie chimed in.

"That's because you're the one who told me," Lagoona responded with a laugh.

"Oh, of course," Frankie said with a sigh. "Sorry. I was so worried I barely slept last night. I can't help but wonder who they'll try to take next."

Just then a hush fell over the Creepateria as Headmistress Bloodgood's horse Nightmare pranced through the doorway. Tall and regal with a shiny blue coat of fur and a bright purple mane and tail, the horse instantly grabbed the whole room's attention. And though the animal was normally a nervous Nelly, today she exuded unwavering confidence. Even the erratic jerking of her lead by the two trolls guiding her into

the Creepateria failed to startle Nightmare. The surprising change in behavior was the sole silver lining in Headmistress Bloodgood's disappearance. So preoccupied was the horse with aiding in her master's return that she simply didn't have time to think about her own problems.

"This is the first time Nightmare's ever let anyone other than Headmistress Bloodgood ride her," Robecca mumbled as she stared up at a young ghoul atop the creature's back.

Operetta, daughter of the Phantom of the Opera, appeared very much at ease on the horse. Dressed in jeans and a sparkly checkered shirt, the ghoul had a distinctive retro flair, especially where her hair was concerned. Styled in 1950s victory curls with short straight bangs, her cherry-

colored locks were hard to miss. So was the heart-shaped rhinestone-encrusted music note around her eye.

"Hey y'all, I'm here today to share a song I wrote about Headmistress Bloodgood—the heart and soul of Monster High," Operetta called out to the Creepateria.

As students and staff members murmured quietly to each other, Operetta slid gracefully off Nightmare's blue back, removed her red guitar from the saddlebag, and flung it over her shoulder.

"Paragraph 58.5 of the Gargoyle Code of Ethics states that it is imprudent to have livestock or horses in the same room as food," Rochelle whispered to Venus and Robecca. "I don't want anyone to get sick, so I ought to say something to Madame Sue Nami, *n'est-ce pas*?"

"Only if you don't mind everyone getting mad at you for ruining the concert," Robecca replied, nudging Venus to say something.

"I think you should keep the information to yourself," Venus instructed Rochelle. "After all, the horse does belong to Headmistress Bloodgood. And you know how much everyone here misses her."

"Point taken," Rochelle said with a nod as Operetta took to a small red stage assembled in the corner of the Creepateria. And though the structure had been built only the night before, there were already silky spider strands billowing from its edges.

"Hey, ghouls and boys, as much as I'd like to sing my new song 'Give Us Back Our Rockin' Headmistress, Normies' live, I can't," Operetta

said, referring to her voice's ability to drive listeners into a state of craziness.

The purple-skinned ghoul then pressed Play on a portable boom box on the stage and began strumming her guitar.

"*She's the heart and soul of this school, a stellar lady who is über cool,*" Operetta lip-synched to the prerecorded track.

"She sure does have a smooth voice," Robecca muttered.

"And she's *trés* gifted on the guitar," Rochelle added.

"*So give us back our rockin' headmistress, normies!*"

"Look at everyone's faces; the song is really affecting them," Venus said as she noted all the misty eyes.

"Thank you, thank you very much!" Operetta called out upon finishing the song. "Now if you'll excuse me, it's time for my fried peanut-butter-and-banana sandwich."

"I miss Headmistress Bloodgood," Frankie blubbered as she wiped tears off her mint-green cheeks.

"Me too," Draculaura mumbled emotionally as she embraced Frankie.

"I feel like my heart was swallowed by a shark," Lagoona Blue said as she shook her head. "The current better change soon, because we need Headmistress Bloodgood. We need her to stop this walling off nonsense. I mean, don't the normies understand that sea creatures can't be landlocked?"

"That song would have been so much better if

I had sung it. I'm, like, a super claw-some singer,"
Toralei bragged while seated arm in arm with
Cleo.

"Claw-some? More like clawful," the mummy
responded cuttingly.

"I won't let them take you," Hoodude cried as
he flung his arms around Frankie.

"Thanks, Hoodude," the green ghoul mumbled.
"But what will you do when they lock us in?"

"I realize this goes against everything you
believe in, Rochelle, but I think we need to head
up to the attic even if it means being late for class.
We need to find out what's on those other papers.
We need to get to the bottom of whatever Miss
Flapper and her cohorts are planning," Venus said,
motioning at their rattled classmates. "Monster
High needs us."

"You are indeed correct; being late to class goes against everything I believe in. But as with the horse in the Creepateria, I feel the extenuating circumstances warrant an exception," Rochelle responded solemnly.

"I guess that means we're heading up to the attic . . . again," Robecca mumbled nervously as the trio headed toward the Creepateria door.

CHAPTER
nine

as the bell rang, signaling the end of lunch, Robecca, Rochelle, and Venus stealthily made their way to the attic stairwell. With the memory of their classmates' fear fresh in their minds, the ghouls slowly mounted the cold stone steps. Silently each hoped for the same thing—that Wydowna would be out. For if she wasn't, they hadn't a clue what their next step would be.

Seconds after Rochelle sliced through the

webbing and popped her head into the attic, she returned with a massive grin. Relieved, Venus and Robecca quickly followed Rochelle into the whimsical little room. Once again enchanted by the craftsmanship, the ghouls took a few seconds to marvel at the finely woven items around them.

"Come on," Venus instructed the others, "we may not have much time."

The jade-skinned ghoul then carefully tucked her vines into her sleeve, pulled back the carpet, and started feeling around the wooden floor for a loose board.

"Got it," she exclaimed just seconds later, and lifted a piece of wood in the air.

"I don't understand," Robecca sputtered, looking into the secret hiding space.

166

"Neither do I," Venus mumbled as she picked up a solitary sheet of paper. "There were at least six or seven pages here last time."

"*Évidemment* she's since moved them or thrown them away," Rochelle answered as she bent down to inspect the dark little trove. "*Boo-la-la*, I don't believe my eyes."

"Then let us look!" Robecca squealed.

Rochelle then pulled a strip of coral fabric off a splintered piece of the floorboard and presented it to Venus and Robecca.

"Miss Flapper's torn dress," Venus muttered. "A normie tried to kidnap her, my foot! She ripped her dress up here and then used the incident to concoct the kidnapping story!"

"I think this is not a hiding spot but a drop box. Wydowna and Miss Flapper communicate by

167

leaving notes in here," Rochelle explained as she accidentally frayed the small piece of fabric with her sharp nails.

"But why communicate through notes when they can just as easily speak face-to-face?" Robecca wondered.

"There is always a certain amount of risk that comes with meeting in person. They could be overheard or seen together. Plus, they keep very different schedules," Rochelle explained as Venus bent down and grabbed the piece of paper.

"'There is to be a meeting on Thursday at 12:01 AM behind the thick grove of conifur trees. Watch us carefully,'" Venus read aloud.

"Watch *us*?" Rochelle repeated. "That implies that whoever wrote this letter will also be attending the meeting. Otherwise he or she

would have simply said, watch *them*."

"Jeepers, what do we think this meeting is about?" Robecca babbled nervously.

"I don't know, but come tomorrow night at 12:01 AM, we're going to find out," Venus answered.

"Come, ghouls, let's get out of here before she returns," Rochelle said as she made her way toward the door. "If we rush we can still make it to Home Ick on time."

After finishing Home Ick and the rest of their classes, the trio grabbed a quick bite in the Creepateria and then headed back to the Chamber of Gore and Lore. And though they were all three relieved to have a lead, they wished they didn't have to wait over twenty-four hours to follow it.

"Venus, I've been thinking about Chewy a great deal lately," Rochelle said as she climbed into bed.

"I'm glad someone else has finally realized how blooming cool my little plant man is," Venus said as she gave Chewy a quick splash of water and a wink.

"I think we should send him to Cy's optometrist. A pair of glasses might help him distinguish food from friend. Or to be more precise, food from Roux and Penny," Rochelle expounded with a smile, sure that this idea would prove helpful to all involved.

"Rochelle, Rochelle, Rochelle," Venus repeated dramatically as she put down the watering can and looked over at her pajama-clad friend. "Chewy has gone through approximately eight pairs of glasses in his life, four of which I can confirm were his."

"*Je ne comprends pas*. What do you mean, 'gone through'?" Rochelle asked.

170

"I think she means he ate them," Robecca explained, tucking a sour-faced Penny next to her in bed.

The sun had barely risen when the soft rustle of a paper passing beneath the door to the Chamber of Gore and Lore caused Robecca to sit straight up in bed. Instantly, the familiar sensation of being late for something she couldn't quite remember took hold. Steam pumped from her ears as she jumped out of bed. However, so sleepy was the copper ghoul that she accidentally knocked her mechanical penguin to the floor. And as Penny was crafted from metal the fall

was rather noisy, waking up both Rochelle and Venus.

"Plants need sleep," Venus griped from beneath her straw eye mask.

"You're not late!" Rochelle called out, her eyes still shut. "*S'il ghoul plaît*, go back to bed!"

After nearly two semesters of rooming with Robecca, both Rochelle and Venus had become accustomed to her many time deficiencies.

"Jumping Jupiter! I was about to oil myself up and race to class!" Robecca exclaimed as she shook her head and wondered if she would ever have a functioning internal clock.

"Sleep . . . is . . . very . . . important . . . to . . . plants. . . ." Venus hummed, still tucked tightly into bed.

"What's that?" Robecca said upon seeing a

piece of paper on the floor. "Someone slipped us a note."

"A note!" Venus cried as she popped out of bed. "Notes at Monster High haven't proven to be a very good thing as of late!"

"*Je suis d'accord*, I agree," Rochelle said as she threw back her covers.

Huddled together by the door, Rochelle and Venus watched as Robecca slowly unfolded the crisp piece of paper.

"The tension is driving me *complètement timbré*! Absolutely crazy! *S'il ghoul plaît*, just open the note already," Rochelle instructed Robecca.

"'Dear Frightingales, as previously discussed, we ask that all members wear Clawdeen's Got Bloodgood T-shirts for Picture Day. And though

we very much hoped our headmistress would be home by now, she is not. So let us wear these shirts as a testament to how much we miss her. Sincerely, Draculaura and Frankie, Copresidents of the Frightingale Society.'"

"I can't believe Picture Day is already here," Venus said as Roux pranced around her feet.

"And we still don't haven't the faintest idea where Headmistress Bloodgood is being kept," Robecca said with steaming nostrils.

"Who knows? Perhaps we'll find out at tonight's meeting," Rochelle added.

"Jeez Louise, you don't think one of our friend's parents has something to do with Headmistress Bloodgood's disappearance, do you?" Robecca asked her friends.

"I don't know. And it might not just be one of

them; it could be all of them. As of now, there's no way of telling," Venus replied.

Though the mood was still uneasy at Monster High, the style-conscious ghouls and guys did their utmost to look defrightful on Picture Day. Frankie re-stitched her limbs using a silky silver thread that glistened beautifully in the sunlight. Draculaura slept with a whitener on her teeth so that she would have a crisp smile. Yellow teeth, especially fangs, were a pet peeve of many vampires, but no one more so than Draculaura. She was adamant that yellow did not

complement her alabaster skin or pink-and-black hair.

Lagoona used a seaweed mask and salt scrub, leaving her face soft and dewy, as though she'd just walked out of the ocean. Hoodude tightened the strings to his button eyes, essentially giving himself a mini face-lift. Rose and Blanche Van Sangre slept an extra hour, for they believed nothing was better for beauty than slumber. The pumpkin heads greased their jack-o'-lanterns with oil so that they would sparkle in the photos. Cleo wrapped herself in new gold-colored gauze. Toralei combed her fur for an extra twenty minutes. Operetta buffed her rhinestone eyepiece. And Deuce exfoliated the snakes on his Mohawk.

Salem's most prestigious photographer, ghost CeeCee Thrue, offered to shoot Monster High's

class portraits in light of the dire circumstances in town. And though no one would accuse her of being a particularly softhearted ghoul, she wanted to give the students of Monster High something wonderful to look back on after the normies walled off the town.

Dressed in head-to-toe black leather, and sporting bright red lipstick and dangly gold earrings, CeeCee looked more like a rock star than a photographer, which just so happened to be exactly how she saw herself.

"Hey! You over there!" CeeCee barked while snapping her fingers. "I need a no foam, nonfat latte with a sprinkle of cinnamon on top. And if they don't have nonfat milk they can mix one part whole milk with two parts water. But only if it's filtered water. Because I don't drink tap, got it?"

"Adult entity, I am the acting headmistress of this school, not your personal assistant," Miss Sue Nami responded as CeeCee began setting up on the front lawn of Monster High.

"I'm not listening to you. But don't take it personally. I don't listen to anyone except myself. Oh, and I need that latte stat, pronto, like five minutes ago. Got it? Good. Later," CeeCee uttered at a rapid-fire pace before turning to assemble her tripod.

Irritated by the fast-talking photographer, Miss Sue Nami stomped off, knocking two zombies and a sea creature out of her way in the process. For if there was one thing Miss Sue Nami didn't like, it was being told what to do by anyone other than Headmistress Bloodgood.

Pounding up the front steps of the school, the

damp woman paused at the sight of Robecca, Rochelle, and Venus encircled by greasy grumbling trolls.

"For the last time, let us pass," Venus huffed as the trolls shook their heads, sending their dirty locks flying.

"It you three! We see you! You in big trouble! We tell Scariff Fred!" a troll hollered, his grubby little cheeks softly shaking.

CHAPTER
ten

first that ghastly ghost and now troll trouble!"
Miss Sue Nami grunted as she approached
the swarm of stout beasts surrounding
Robecca, Rochelle, and Venus.

"Miss Sue Nami!" Robecca yelped with steam
bubbling out of her ears. "Please help us! These
trolls won't listen! And I'm worried that if they
don't back off soon they'll ruin our special Got
Bloodgood T-shirts!"

"Trolls? You work for me. So that means you

need to tell me exactly what this is about," Miss Sue Nami ordered, her hands perched atop her hips.

"They steal from Monster High! Robbers! Bad ghouls!"

"Steal?" Miss Sue Nami repeated back incredulously.

"Yeah, Hairy saw them sneaking out of attic stairwell a couple nights ago," one of the trolls said while waving his hand in Rochelle's face.

"I would be more than happy to donate nail brushes and files if you lot are willing to use them," Rochelle said, cringing at the gross state of the troll's nails.

"Non-adult entities, is this true? Are you stealing from your own school?"

"*Non! Absolument pas!*" Rochelle stated ser-

iously, clearly offended by the accusation. "A gargoyle has not been accused of stealing in three centuries! This is *complètement* absurd!"

"So you were never in the attic stairwell? You're saying that Hairy is mistaken? That perhaps his thick follicles clouded his vision? Or that he is just a plain old fibber?" Miss Sue Nami questioned the three ghouls.

"Well . . ." Robecca uttered nervously.

"Yes, we were in the attic stairwell, but we didn't steal anything," Venus explained.

"The attic stairwell is off-limits to non-adult entities. So what exactly prompted you three to break rules and risk detention in the no-fungeon?"

Venus paused and pursed her lips as she decided how much to share with Miss Sue Nami. For while the damp dame had proven herself a

skeptic of Miss Flapper, Venus didn't think it smart to create conjecture. She decided it far more sensible to wait until they had a firm grasp on what was happening.

"We were in the stairwell because Penny, Robecca's pet penguin, ran away," Venus blurted out.

"What?!" Robecca screamed emotionally, reacting to Venus's comment before realizing that it was nothing more than a tall tale to cover up their outing. "What . . . transpired was very stressful for me. I couldn't find my dear beloved pet for almost . . . twenty minutes."

"Which may not sound like a long time, but it certainly felt like a long time," Rochelle added. "Especially for a ghoul without a functioning internal clock."

"Very well, then. Trolls, you may let them pass," Miss Sue Nami grunted. "Non-adult entities, let it be known, if I catch you in the attic stairwell again, you'll be spending the next semester in the no-fungeon."

"Yes, of course, Madame Sue Nami," Rochelle answered guiltily, for if there was one thing she didn't like it was fibbing.

"Oh, and I don't like that photographer ghost . . . not one bit," Miss Sue Nami added with a particularly grumpy expression.

"Do you think she's *dangereuse*?" Rochelle asked as she nervously furrowed her brow.

"No, just irritating. Sort of like a beaver," Miss Sue Nami griped under her breath.

"A what?" Rochelle inquired curiously.

"You know, those pesky little animals with

185

long teeth, flat tails, and a proclivity for building dams, which cause rivers to overflow," Miss Sue Nami explained before abruptly stomping off.

CeeCee Thrue began each sitting in the same brusque manner. She eyed the monster up and down, pulled at their clothes, fussed with their hair, and occasionally even removed or applied makeup. Within seconds of seeing a ghoul or guy, she knew what their best angle was, how to light them, whether they should show fangs, and so on. However talented she was, CeeCee was also impatient, self-absorbed, and at times even rude.

"Lose the jacket, look to the left, relax your fin, raise your right eyebrow, smooth your scales, smile less, smile more, freeze," CeeCee rattled off

before snapping a couple of pictures. "Okay, get up! Go! Next!"

"Hello, Ms. Thrue, it's such a pleasure to meet you. I'm Frankie Stein, copresident of the Frightingale Society and—"

"Sit down, you emerald in the rough. You need to be polished. Stat. Pull back your hair. Wipe off your lip gloss."

"But—"

"They distract from your greenness, and the only thing better than green is gold. Move two inches to the left. Half an inch to the right."

"What?"

"Don't talk. Close your mouth. Smile. Okay, got it. That's it. Now go!" CeeCee instructed firmly, motioning for the next candidate.

"It sure is the cat's pajamas to meet a

photographer of your caliber, or really of any caliber. You see, when I was disassembled, cameras hadn't even been invented yet," Robecca said as she took a seat on the stool.

"Put that copper thing down—"

"Copper thing? Oh, you mean Penny. But she isn't a copper *thing* at all, she's my *friend* and she absolutely loves having her picture taken. Not that you can tell, since she's always frowning, but believe me, it's true."

"Lose the copper thing. Buff your nose. Tighten the rivet on your right knee. Put your left hand under your chin."

"What was that? You're talking so fast that I can barely understand you!" Robecca babbled frantically.

"Right hand on hip, left hand under chin, eyes wide. That's it. Got it. Next!"

Though it had only been a few minutes, Robecca had already forgotten about Penny. In fact, had she not tripped over the small metal bird while stepping off the stool, she most definitely would have left her behind. And if there was one thing that made Penny's frown deepen, it was getting left behind.

With Penny again tucked tightly beneath her right arm, Robecca walked over to where Rochelle and Venus were waiting. However, just before she reached her friends she saw a sign with the acronym GHOOL (Get Heels Off of Lawn). Instantly her pistons began pumping as an idea took hold in her mind. What if Asome wasn't the name of the head of the mysterious society or even the

189

society itself, but an acronym for the society's name?

"Ghouls! What if A-S-O-M-E is an acronym?" Robecca blurted out as she bounded up to Rochelle and Venus.

"It is, of course, possible," said Rochelle. "But unless you have an idea what the acronym is, then we don't really have much to go on."

"Deary me, and here I thought I had experienced an epiphany!" Robecca said with disappointment.

"More like half an epiphany," Venus joked. "How was having your portrait taken?"

"CeeCee Thrue might be a celebrated photographer, but she has a terrible bedside manner," Robecca said while shaking her head. "She's worse than a porcupine with a balloon."

"In CeeCee's defense, perhaps her bedside manner isn't very good because there isn't a bed in sight," Rochelle pointed out.

"Rochelle, Rochelle," Venus muttered under her breath.

"Yes, Venus, Venus," Rochelle replied just as CeeCee waved her over.

After eyeing the hard-bodied ghoul, CeeCee picked up the stool and placed it a few feet away.

"No sitting for you. Gargoyles always break my stools. Now relax your shoulders. Polish your cheeks. Come on, ghoul, act alive," CeeCee barked rapidly.

"I'm afraid I cannot *act* alive as I *am* alive. A fact which I thought you of all monsters would know, seeing as you're a ghost, a non-living creature," Rochelle replied.

"Put both of your hands over your mouth," CeeCee instructed the loquacious ghoul.

"Like this?" Rochelle asked, her voice muffled by her thick stone hands.

"Great. Got it. Good-bye."

"*S'il ghoul plaît,* Madame Thrue. I cannot have a class photo with my hands across my mouth," Rochelle pleaded with the photographer.

"Next!"

"Madame Thrue—"

"Next!"

"The Gargoyle Code of Ethics states that the customer is always correct except of course when he or she is wrong, which does not apply in this scenario. So might I ask you to retake my picture?"

"Next!"

"Very well, then, you have given me no choice but to write a highly unflattering review on Deadslist!"

Later that day, as the ghouls chatted over dinner in the Creepateria, a murmur started in the far corner of the room. And though it began relatively calmly, by the time it reached Robecca, Rochelle, and Venus, it had morphed into a hysterical shriek.

"Miss Flapper found a letter under her door warning that next time she wouldn't get away! That none of us would ever get away again, not after the wall is built!" Frankie squealed with terror to Draculaura.

"What are we going to do? Monster High, and even the whole town of Salem, isn't strong enough to fight the normies! I don't care what my parents say. I don't think Scariff Fred realizes what we're up against!" Draculaura exclaimed while pulling at her pigtails nervously.

"I am sad to say, I think you're right," Miss Flapper added in her usual soft-spoken manner. "We're going to need help to battle the normies."

"My hair! My poor hair! It will never be this shiny again! There's no way the normies will let us have high-gloss products!"

"*Pardonnez-moi*, Madame Flapper," Rochelle called out to the chicly dressed dragon. "But might we see the letter?"

"I'm terribly sorry, but I already gave it to Scariff

194

Fred," Miss Flapper replied, turning to leave. "Oh, and I would be careful, ghouls, for as I told Scariff Fred, they're watching us . . . preparing for their next move. . . ."

As soon as Miss Flapper had floated out of earshot, Venus motioned for Robecca and Rochelle to lean in.

"She's raising the stakes, making sure everyone is scared," Venus declared before releasing a long, drawn-out sigh.

"We need to find out what she's planning. Time is running out," Rochelle exclaimed while tapping her claws against her hard stone cheek.

"Maybe we'll find out at tonight's meeting," Robecca offered. "Although, am I the only one who thinks meeting in the woods after midnight sounds like the beginning of a scary movie?"

A full moon hung low in the sky, casting silver beams of light down through the thick conifur branches. Crickets chirping, bugs digging, and bats flapping turned the wooded area behind the school into a veritable symphony of sounds. Listening from their camouflaged post beneath a mass of fallen branches were Robecca, Rochelle, Venus, and Cy.

Venus, Rochelle, and Cy carefully monitored their watches, waiting dutifully for the hand to strike midnight and then 12:01 AM. Robecca, on the other hand, never one for time or timeliness, had fallen asleep while tucked beneath

the prickly conifur branches. But as the ghoul had copper skin, she hardly had to worry about scratches.

"Robecca's fast asleep," Cy whispered to Rochelle and Venus. "And it's almost time. Should I wake her?"

"Nah. Let her sleep. We already have five eyes and six ears, what's another two more of each going to do?" Venus explained as she heard the familiar sound of feet sinking into piles of dried leaves.

First to arrive was Ghoulia's mother, Mrs. Yelps, who in typical zombie fashion moved at an extremely slow pace. Next to appear on the scene was the well-coiffed duo Mr. and Mrs. Wolf, whose locks glistened beautifully in the moonlight. Trailing immediately behind the couple was Mr.

Stein, whose limbs created quite a ruckus as he stomped through the forest. Seconds later, as if out of nowhere, Dracula appeared, dramatically throwing open his cape.

"What are you doing in a cape?" Mrs. Wolf giggled. "It's a little cliché, don't you think?"

"I know, but it was either this or my robe. As you know, I have very little black clothing in my wardrobe," Mr. Dracula explained as Mr. De Nile approached in a dark black suit with a small sphinx cat perched on his shoulder.

"Seriously, Ramses? You brought your cat?" Mr. Stein scoffed.

"That's Your Royal Highness to you," Mr. De Nile replied arrogantly.

"More like Your Royal Heinous," Mr. Stein joked under his breath.

"That is not funny," Ramses blustered. "A lineage such as mine deserves better than your poor attempts at humor."

"We don't have much time," Mr. Wolf pointed out as beams of red and blue light began to ricochet through the thick conifur trees.

"What's happening?" Venus whispered to Cy and Rochelle.

But before either could answer, a blaring siren swept through the air, piercing the eardrums of everyone within a hundred-yard radius.

"Cover Robecca's mouth!" Venus ordered Rochelle.

"But my hands are dirty!"

"Where am—" Robecca stammered as her eyes popped open.

Ever the vigilant friend to Robecca, Cy threw

his soft white hand across her cold copper lips. Within seconds, Monster High was swarming with black-and-white scariff cars.

"Disband! Disband!" Mr. Wolf whispered as he grabbed his wife's hand and dashed off into the woods.

As the lights and siren continued, Mr. De Nile, Mrs. Yelps, Mr. Stein, and Dracula quickly followed suit and disappeared into the grove of trees.

"Look, there's Scariff Fred and Superintendent Petra," Cy whispered, his hand still covering Robecca's mouth.

"What could possibly bring Scariff Fred, Superintendent Petra, and all those officers out here at this hour?" Rochelle pondered while repeatedly rubbing her chin.

"Something important . . ." Venus muttered.

"By the looks of it, I think we're about to find out," Cy said as Scariff Fred and a battalion of officers stormed through the front doors of the school.

CHAPTER
eleven

blue and red lights flashed frenetically against the dark sky. Car radios crackled loudly, echoing through the windless night. Slowly pacing in front of the main entrance to Monster High was a group of three or four deputies who were all zombies.

"Can you imagine one of those zombies chasing down a criminal?" Venus asked, watching them sluggishly drag their feet.

"I think it's safe to say the scariff puts

werewolves and other more energetic monsters in charge of the chasing," Cy responded.

"Is it possible the scariff has finally caught on to Miss Flapper? That he's here to arrest her?" Robecca asked her friends hopefully.

"*C'est possible*," Rochelle replied. "Or perhaps they are here because they found out where Headmistress Bloodgood is stashed away."

"Wouldn't that be the bee's knees? Why, just the thought of seeing good old headless Headmistress Bloodgood makes my pistons pump!"

The sound of feet stomping preceded the throng of deputies exiting the main entrance. Two, then four, then six, then eight, then ten uniformed monsters stomped down the steps.

"Where's Scariff Fre—" Venus was starting to ask when she spotted the scariff. Or precisely, she

saw his ample belly, soon followed by the rest of him. Walking next to Scariff Fred was a lithe figure with bright orange hair and six hands, all of which were handcuffed behind her back.

"It's the spider ghoul," Cy mumbled at the sight of Wydowna.

"Does this mean Scariff Fred has figured out whom she's working with?" Robecca asked.

"I don't think so. If that were the case they would have arrested Miss Flapper too," Venus stated as she watched Scariff Fred put Wydowna into the back of his car.

"Madame Flapper is a very smart woman. I wouldn't be surprised if she used her wiles to put all the blame on Wydowna," Rochelle said as she tapped her claws against a twig, creating a small pile of sawdust in the process.

One by one, the scariff cars pulled away from Monster High, once again leaving the school cloaked in the darkness of night. Unsure what to make of the evening, or what to do next, the quartet made their way back into the school.

"If only the bats could tell us what they saw," Robecca muttered as she looked up at the small black creatures hunting for prey.

"I say we check out the attic," Venus declared boldly.

"*Mais, non!* They didn't take Madame Flapper, so it is highly probable that she is up there right now," Rochelle pointed out logically.

"Yeah, destroying information," Venus muttered while shaking her head in frustration.

Boom, splash, boom, splash! Dressed in an unflattering plastic robe and a shower cap, Miss Sue Nami turned the corner and bumped straight into the foursome.

"Non-adult entities, leaving the dormitory at night is strictly against school policy. And you know how I feel about school policy."

"*S'il ghoul plaît*, Madame Sue Nami, you know how seriously I take rules. Dare I say, even more seriously than you? After all, I have an entire code of ethics, whereas you only have a few pages of school rules," Rochelle expounded.

"Rochelle, I'm thinking now is not the best time to compete for who has the most rules," Venus counseled the hardheaded ghoul.

"All four of you are to return to the dorm-itory this second," Miss Sue Nami ordered.

"But it is impossible for us to get to the dormitory *this second*. We are going to need at least *thirty to forty seconds* to make it to our rooms," Rochelle replied in her most matter-of-fact manner.

"If I didn't have a more pressing matter to attend to, I would write you all up for detention!" Miss Sue Nami grumbled.

"You mean the spider ghoul in the attic?" Venus inquired.

"How do you know about her?" Miss Sue Nami asked, her eyes widening with curiosity.

"We followed the webs to the attic," Venus answered.

"Smart, very smart," Miss Sue Nami said as she broke into a dog shake. However, as the

waterlogged woman was wearing both a shower cap and a plastic robe, it was nowhere near as dampening as usual.

"That photographer with all the attitude . . ." Miss Sue Nami grunted.

"CeeCee Thrue," Cy chimed in.

"Yeah, that's her," Miss Sue Nami said with a nod. "When she started developing the portraits, she noticed a pair of eyes peering out of the attic window. She notified the scariff immediately. And in light of Miss Flapper's letter from the normies this afternoon, Scariff Fred decided not to take any chances, so he came right over and grabbed her."

"Do you know what she was doing in the attic? Is it possible that it has something to do with Headmistress Bloodgood's disappearance?" Rochelle asked.

"The scariff thinks she's a normie spy," Miss Sue Nami explained. "Now, for the last time, go back to the dormitory!"

"Okay, but where are you going?" Venus wondered.

"The scariff's department to get more information."

"Dressed like that? *Boo-la-la*," Rochelle said as she shook her head at Miss Sue Nami's robe and shower cap. "Surely there's time for you to change into something more appropriate."

"Watch it," Miss Sue Nami grunted as she stomped away.

After bidding good night to Cy, the three ghouls headed to their room in the dormitory.

"I'm so tired I almost feel like a Van Sangre sister," Robecca mumbled as she yawned.

"Please don't say their names," Venus moaned. "I am too exhausted to even think about those two."

"Ghoulfriends, I am sorry to tell you, but fatigue is a well-known reason for underachievement, which does not bode well for our quiz in Catacombing tomorrow," Rochelle worried.

"We have bigger issues than a test, Rochelle," Venus explained as she grabbed hold of the doorknob to the Chamber of Gore and Lore.

"Like what?" a soft voice whispered in the darkness.

Stepping out of the shadows was the always-ravishing Miss Flapper. Dressed in powder-blue pajamas, the European dragon somehow still managed to look elegant.

"Um," Robecca mumbled nervously, steam

pouring out of her nostrils, "Penny was recently diagnosed with rusted gears. She's going to need major surgery at Grind 'n' Gears."

"Yeah, we're all super worried," Venus fibbed, nervously playing with her vines.

"Well then, *bonsoir*, Madame Flapper," Rochelle blurted out in an attempt to end the conversation.

"I'm so sorry to hear about Penny. But just one more thing before you go, ghouls. What are you doing out at such a late hour?" Miss Flapper asked with a tense smile.

"We needed a snack," Venus mumbled.

"But the Creepateria's closed," Miss Flapper responded with growing intensity.

"Yes, but I keep roasted nuts and seeds in my locker, so we went downstairs for an impromptu picnic," Venus babbled unconvincingly as she

pushed open the door to their dormitory room and pulled Rochelle and Robecca in after her.

"Good night!" Robecca called out as the door to the Chamber of Gore and Lore slammed shut.

CHAPTER twelve

by the time Monster High's first bell rang the following morning, the whole school was abuzz with nerves over the purported normie spy in the attic.

"*Normie spies in our school! They're turning us into fools! Normie spies in our school! They're turning us into fools!*" the pumpkin heads sang as they bounced down the busy hall.

"How is it possible that they turned one of our own against us? That the normies convinced a monster to spy on another monster! That's

just wrong!" Lagoona groused to Frankie and Draculaura with a furrowed brow.

"All I can say is Salem is in trouble, like high-voltage trouble," Frankie announced seriously.

"What if the normies refuse to let me have my iron shakes? Without them . . . oh, I can't even bear to think about it," Draculaura trailed off as everyone's iCoffins dinged.

LISTEN UP, GHOULS AND GUYS. I JUST HEARD THAT THE SPIDER CREATURE FOUND IN THE ATTIC IS NOT A NORMIE SPY AFTER ALL. THE EIGHT-ARMED GHOUL GOES BY THE NAME WYDOWNA SPIDER AND CLAIMS TO HAVE BEEN HIDING IN THE ATTIC SO SHE COULD EAVESDROP ON CLASSES TO LEARN. WHEN ASKED WHY SHE DIDN'T JUST APPLY TO THE SCHOOL LIKE OTHER MONSTERS, SHE SAID SHE HAD BEEN TOLD THAT MONSTER HIGH WAS NOT ACCEPTING ANY NEW STUDENTS.

216

P.S. CRACK AND SHIELD DAY IS NOW ONLY THREE DAYS AWAY, SO GET READY, GET SET, AND START STRETCHING!

While Spectra's blog post calmed the bubbling hysteria in the hallways, there was no denying that everyone was more than a little apprehensive of Wydowna. The simple fact that she had been hiding, spying on them from the air vents, left the students feeling ill at ease and unusually unfriendly.

So much so that when the scariff returned her to Monster High, few outside of Frankie and Draculaura would even smile at the ghoul, let alone speak to her. And when it came to housing

in the dormitory, Miss Sue Nami decided it best she be given a single room. However, without roommates, the acting headmistress recognized that she might need some assistance and so she asked Robecca, Rochelle, and Venus to show Wydowna around. This suited the trio fine since they were eager to gather information on the ghoul.

"So you were just living in the attic and listening to our classes?" Venus asked Wydowna as she, Robecca, and Rochelle made their way down the main hall toward the elevator to the Catacombs.

"What can I say? I like to study," Wydowna answered with a tight smile.

"And yet we saw no textbooks or notebooks in the attic?" Rochelle asked in an interrogatory tone.

"You've been to the attic?" Wydowna asked, clearly startled.

"No! Um, of course not," Robecca jumped in. "Rochelle meant to say that we *heard* that there weren't any books and stuff in the attic."

"I don't need to read or write anything down. I remember everything I hear and see. Spiders have very good memories, you know," Wydowna explained.

"What a shame," Robecca blurted out, prompting Venus and Rochelle to look at her quizzically. "Oh, I only meant that with six arms you'd be a great note taker. Not like me; I'm always steaming up my papers by accident."

Venus pushed the button to summon the elevator to the Catacombs, just as Cleo and Toralei sauntered up.

"I never thought I'd say this, but what are you ghouls doing hanging out with her?" Toralei asked before motioning in Wydowna's direction.

"*Pardonnez-moi?*"

"You ghouls are super scratchy and annoying, but she's even worse . . . she's feral," Toralei said, scowling at Wydowna.

"She's not feral!" Venus snapped.

"Well, she was squatting in a building; that sounds pretty feral to me," Toralei hissed.

"Me too," Cleo added before pulling at Toralei's arm. "Someone needs a clawdicure. Like ASAP!"

"Whatever, gauze head," Toralei retorted as the elevator doors opened.

"We'll wait," Venus said as the golden doors closed.

"Sorry about them," Robecca muttered to

Wydowna. "They're a bit batty . . . and catty . . . and, occasionally, even downright ratty!"

"It's okay; every school has a few ghouls like that," Wydowna said with a smile.

"Did your last school?" Venus inquired while doing her best to feign casualness.

"Of course."

"And where was your last school?" Venus continued.

"Um, um," Wydowna stuttered. "You wouldn't know it. It's in the Old World."

"You came all the way over here from the Old World?" Rochelle asked incredulously.

"What can I say? Monster High has a very good reputation," Wydowna mumbled quietly.

"And you weren't afraid to come here on your own?" Robecca asked.

"No, not at all. I'm actually pretty used to being alone, since it's always been just me and my mom. . . ."

"What about your dad?" Robecca asked as thoughts of her own father passed through her mind.

"My mom, Arachne, was a normie until Athena turned her into a black widow. . . . And black widows don't really like to keep guys around, so I never had a chance to get to know my father."

"But I imagine you and your *maman* are very close since it's just the two of you," Rochelle added.

"Yeah, but she's super busy. I don't get to see her that much. It's okay, because I have Shoo and she's great company. Well, except that she can't talk."

"And thank heavens for that," Venus muttered,

remembering that Shoo watched her tiptoe out of the attic.

"Excuse me?" Wydowna replied.

"Oh, I just meant that talking pets would be such a headache, more annoying than a case of root rot, if you know what I mean," Venus blathered nervously as the group stepped onto the elevator to the Catacombs.

Later that evening in the Creepateria, Robecca, Rochelle, and Venus whispered quietly to each other over dinner. Wydowna, exhausted after her first full day of actually attending classes, had decided to go straight to bed.

"Wydowna seems so nice. It's hard to believe she's caught up with Miss Flapper and all this other stuff," Robecca said as she pushed her casketdilla around on her plate.

"I know what you mean. But the facts are the facts. She's working with Miss Flapper and this secret group. They took Headmistress Bloodgood and they're blaming it on the normies. So no matter how nice she may seem, there's obviously more to her," Venus declared before taking a bite of her casketdilla.

"I think we must be as kind as possible with Wydowna in order to earn her trust," Rochelle suggested.

"Agreed," Venus replied.

"Now then, do you think it inappropriate if I ask her to weave something for me?"

Rochelle asked seriously.

"Rochelle," Venus droned as she shook her head.

"I take it that's a no," Rochelle said as she bowed her head, slightly ashamed. "She's just so talented!"

For once, it was not the shrieks of Robecca thinking she was late that stirred Venus and Rochelle in the middle of the night. Instead it was the sound of a muffled voice coming through the wall. And though it was nearly impossible to decipher the words, it was clear that it was Miss Flapper and that she was angry. One by one, the trio tiptoed across the room and pressed their copper, stone,

and green ears to the wall. And though they tried with all their might to hear what Miss Flapper was saying, it was too garbled to make out more than the occasional word.

"I think it's safe to assume that she's talking to Wydowna," Rochelle whispered.

"And why do you suppose she's so angry at Wydowna?" Robecca asked with Penny cradled in her metallic arms.

"I suspect that being caught in CeeCee's pictures was not part of their plan," Rochelle said as they heard the soft sound of a door opening.

Moving faster than fire on a dried-out fern, Venus darted to the door and cracked it open a sliver. The green ghoul then positioned her head so she could see Wydowna standing in the

hall. However, try as she did to catch a glimpse of Miss Flapper, Venus could only hear her.

"Never forget that you are but a servant executing a plan, Wydowna. Your loyalty is to your master. You are not to question what they have asked us to do," Miss Flapper whispered softly, and then closed the door on Wydowna.

Standing alone in the hallway with hunched shoulders, Wydowna had such sad eyes that even Venus felt pangs of sorrow and empathy. For in that moment she appeared very much like a little girl lost, far away from home, with neither friends nor family. Overwhelmed with compassion for the ghoul, Venus momentarily contemplated saying something. But then she remembered Headmistress Bloodgood, and her empathy instantly disappeared.

"I don't like the sound of servant or master," Robecca mumbled after Venus closed the door.

"Madame Flapper seems concerned about Wydowna's allegiance. Why else would she remind her about staying loyal to her master? And not questioning the plan?" Rochelle assessed as she tapped her sharp claws against Roux's back.

"Even the smallest break in Wydowna's loyalty gives us an opening, a chance to gain her confidence and sway her allegiance. Then we can ask her about Asome and the plan," Venus suggested as Robecca flung her right index finger in the air.

"And where Headmistress Bloodgood is; Monster High needs her back!"

229

CHAPTER
thirteen

Crack and Shield Day's Opening Scaremony was quite the affair. The shrill team shrieked in formation as the band played and the Fear Squad cheered. Then, immediately following the performances, Superintendent Petra took to the field with a torch in her right hand. Miss Sue Nami had thought she would stand in for Headmistress Bloodgood, but Superintendent Petra wouldn't hear of it. Apparently she liked the attention that came with being a torchbearer too much. Not that anyone could tell, since her

overuse of Crowtox had left her incapable of showing any emotion.

After making her way halfway around the field, Superintendent Petra passed the torch to Frankie Stein. The well-sewn ghoul then toured around the other half of the field as the student body cheered, delighted that Crack and Shield Day was finally upon them. And not simply because they loved to watch students participate in the Blood Curdling Hurdles or Fifty Eater Sprint, but because the weeks of relentless uncertainty had left everyone desperate for something to celebrate.

As the Opening Scaremony came to an end, the band set up along the edge of the field, where they literally scored the soundtrack to the games. When athletes broke records, horns sounded. When they grew frustrated, violins squeaked. And

when they lost, the baritone bass comforted them.

The first race of the day was the Ghoul's Cry Jump, a competition to see who could simultaneously jump the highest while shrieking the loudest. On the field, ready to participate, were Venus, Robecca, Rochelle, Scarah Screams, Cleo, and Toralei, all of whom were wearing matching Monster High helmets.

"Welcome to Monster High's Twelfth Annual Crack and Shield Day," Miss Sue Nami yelled into a bullhorn. "First up in the Ghoul's Cry Jump is Rochelle Goyle."

Rochelle raised her right hand and waved to the cheering crowd as if she were a visiting dignitary as opposed to an athlete preparing to compete. Seconds later, she was poised at the line, waiting for the starting gun to fire. And when

it did, she took off running as fast as she could, before jumping into the air and screaming at the top of her lungs.

"Holy mackerel, who knew Rochelle had those kind of pipes?" Robecca muttered to Venus, impressed by their friend's shriek.

"I know, right? If only she could get her granite body a little higher in the air," Venus responded.

Next up was Cleo, who along with Toralei was immediately disqualified for refusing to unlink arms. Then came Venus, who proved a surprising front-runner after both shrieking loudly and jumping high. Immediately after Venus, Robecca stepped up to the starting line. However, she concentrated so strongly on her jump that she forgot to scream entirely.

"Venus, I think you might actually take this

one!" Robecca squealed with delight after finishing her jump.

"I am very sorry to say, *chérie,* but I do not think that will happen," Rochelle interrupted. "Scarah Screams is a banshee; she can shriek better than anyone. Plus, I have it on very good authority that she is rather light on her feet."

And as Robecca saw seconds later, Rochelle was most definitely correct in her assessment.

"Sorry, Venus, I know how much second place can sting," Robecca offered sympathetically as they walked off the field.

"We're here to befriend Wydowna, not become the next Usain Thunderbolt," Venus replied as the ghouls made their way over to the timid-looking spider ghoul, standing alone at the edge of the grass.

"Hey, Wydowna!" Robecca called out cheerfully.

"Hi," Wydowna said while keeping her eyes trained on her feet.

"What are you doing over here by yourself?" Rochelle inquired while doing her best to hide her suspicions.

"I'm waiting for the Fifty Eater Sprint while also trying to avoid Cleo and Toralei," Wydowna replied honestly.

"Those two are such a pain. Listening to all that bickering gives me such a headache," Venus commiserated.

"I don't mind that so much, but I do mind some of their remarks," Wydowna explained.

"Oh dear! What have they been saying now?" Robecca asked with genuine concern before reminding herself that Wydowna was supposed to

be one of the bad ghouls responsible for Headmistress Bloodgood's kidnapping.

"Well," Wydowna started to explain, and then paused at the sight of Toralei and Cleo fast approaching.

"Hey, Cleo," Toralei said with a smirk after stopping a few feet from Robecca, Rochelle, Venus, and Wydowna.

"Hey, Toralei."

"Did you hear about that new ghoul? The one who's been leeching off our school, living in the attic, and cavesdropping on us?" Toralei said, staring down Wydowna.

"Aunty Neferia always said that spider ghouls are not to be trusted. That with six hands, they're always doing something behind your back," Cleo sneered.

"Ghouls, cut it out! Stop acting like such *mullies*!" Venus shot back.

Robecca instinctively covered Rochelle's mouth as the granite ghoul prepared to once again tell Venus that *mully* was not an actual word.

"This has nothing to do with you, weed, so why don't you just buzz off," Toralei snapped.

"That's where you're wrong," Robecca jumped in. "If we just stand by and let you treat her like this, then we're no better than you two."

"*C'est vrai*. We are all monsters. We are all created equal. And we all deserve to be treated with respect," Rochelle said after pushing Robecca's hand off of her mouth.

Cleo actually started to look ashamed, but before she could say anything, Toralei jumped in. "You ghouls are wrong about this webbed weirdo,"

the werecat snapped. "And mark my words, you'll be sorry. . . ."

And with that Toralei jerked Cleo's arm, and the two sauntered away.

"You ghouls really shouldn't have gotten involved. It's only going to bring more headaches to the three of you," Wydowna mumbled sadly.

"Don't worry about it; we can handle it," Venus replied firmly.

"I really should get going. I need to stretch out my mouth before the Fifty Eater Sprint." Wydowna said while looking at one of the many watches on her arms.

The Fifty Eater Sprint was one of Crack and Shield's hardest events. It required not only speed on the track but a high-functioning digestive system, for after each ten-foot interval, participants

had to down a bagel with scream cheese.

"Is everything okay over here, ghouls?" Miss Flapper asked after floating over to the group. "I certainly hope our students are making you feel at home here at Monster High, Wydowna."

"Oh yes," Wydowna replied without even looking up at Miss Flapper.

"You know it's almost time for your race. Don't you want to stretch out your mouth?" Miss Flapper asked Wydowna pointedly.

"Yes, that's exactly what I want to do," Wydowna responded before wandering off.

It was nearly the end of Crack and Shield Day before Robecca, Rochelle, and Venus were able to locate Wydowna again. Hiding behind the concession stand with Shoo, the flame-haired ghoul busied herself by weaving a scarf.

"Hey, what are you doing back here? You're about to miss the Sea Creature Swim-Off," Robecca called out to Wydowna.

"Spider ghouls aren't much for water. We're surprisingly bad swimmers, considering how many arms we have," Wydowna said with a slight giggle.

"*Boo-la-la*, Wydowna, you are so talented. I cannot tell you how I envy your ability to create such items," Rochelle gushed over the scarf.

"Thanks," Wydowna said quietly. "You ghouls have been really nice to me."

"Why wouldn't we be? After all, you're a new student at Monster High. I'm only sorry that you've arrived at such a precarious time," Venus explained.

"Venus is, of course, referring to the normie

241

threat," Rochelle clarified while holding Wydowna's gaze.

"Yeah, the scariff mentioned something about that at the station," Wydowna mumbled uncomfortably. "It's terrible what those normies are planning to do."

"Is it?" Venus asked Wydowna sharply. "Or rather, what I meant to say was, are the normies really planning to do something to us?"

"That's what the scariff said, but what do I know? I've only been here a few weeks," Wydowna stammered as she stopped weaving and stood up. "Maybe I *will* catch the Sea Creature Swim-Off, after all."

Venus, Robecca, and Rochelle stepped closer to the ghoul, effectively stopping her cold in her tracks.

"We know what you're doing," Venus pressed Wydowna. "We know who you're working with. We just don't understand why you're doing it."

"I don't know what you mean," Wydowna uttered nervously.

"Stop pretending, Wydowna. It's more irksome than an empty boiler," Robecca snapped.

"I'm not pretending. . . . I don't know," Wydowna whispered as she looked down at Shoo.

"You seem so nice, so genuine. I don't get it. How could you get caught up in something like this? A society that holds some creatures above others? That's not right and you know it," Venus chastised the ghoul.

"You don't understand," Wydowna babbled as she began to cry. "I thought I was being sent here to help monsters. For the good of the whole monster

world. But then I started reading things . . . things I didn't like or even understand. . . ."

"Just tell us who's behind this! What or who is Asome?" Venus pushed the frightened spider ghoul to confess.

"I can't tell you. . . . It's too dangerous. . . ."

"You must tell us! The future of every ghoul and guy at Monster High depends on it!" Rochelle pleaded. "*S'il ghoul plaît*, Wydowna."

"You don't understand how powerful they are," Wydowna stuttered as she started crying louder.

"Just tell us who they are! We can handle them!" Venus screamed, losing her patience.

"You don't get it. You won't be able to stop them!" Wydowna screamed back abruptly.

"We stopped Miss Flapper's Whisper and we're going to stop this too," Venus stated assuredly.

"Don't you see? It's all part of the same plan."

"What plan?" Robecca implored, steam pouring out of her ears.

"You don't have a clue how far up this goes, how long this plan has been in the making," Wydowna said as a loud siren cut through the air.

Seconds later, Superintendent Petra's voice boomed over the loudspeakers on the field.

"This is not a drill. Repeat, this is not a drill. All students and staff members are to report immediately to the gym for lockdown."

"S'il ghoul plait, Wydowna, tell us before it's too late," Rochelle begged as the field erupted in chaos.

"I think it already is. . . ."

To be continued . . .

245

ABOUT THE AUTHOR

As a child Gitty Daneshvari talked and talked and talked. Whether yammering at her sister through a closed door or bombarding her parents with questions while they attempted to sleep, she absolutely refused to stop chattering until finally there was no one left to listen. In need of an outlet for her thoughts, Gitty began writing, and she hasn't stopped since. Gitty is also the author of the middle-grade series *School of Fear.*

She currently lives in New York City with her highly literate English bulldog, Harriet. And yes, she still talks too much.

Visit her at www.gittydaneshvari.com.

Keep a lurk out for the
ghoulfriends' next adventure,
coming soon!

CHAPTER
one

nestled deep within the lush forests of Oregon was a small and seemingly average town. Much like any other town in America, it had shops, restaurants, small family homes, and, of course, schools. So normal was the appearance of the town that it was actually quite forgettable. Every year countless travelers passed through without giving it so much as a second thought, utterly unaware that there was anything extraordinary or unique about the place. But, of course, had anyone stopped for a closer inspection, it would have become readily apparent that the town of Salem catered to a rather specific clientele—monsters!

And while one might think that a town of monsters was terribly intriguing, it wasn't. Salem had long puttered by with nary a scandal or drama outside of the occasional spat over which cemetery would host the Dance of the Delightfully Dead, a celebration of the happily departed. In fact, so unremarkable was the community that the most exciting thing on the horizon was the start of a new semester at Monster High.

Bright and early Monday morning, the well-worn wrought-iron gates to Monster High creaked open to a fast-approaching blitz of bodies. Amid the throngs of monster students was a petite gray gargoyle outfitted in a delightful pink linen dress with a Scaremès scarf wrapped stylishly around her waist as a belt. Moving carefully through the crowd, the young girl minded her Louis Creton luggage and her pet griffin, Roux, but mostly her own two hands. As gargoyles are crafted of stone, they are burdened with both extreme heaviness and terribly sharp claws. And the last thing she wanted to do was snag her dress on the first day at a new school.

"*Pardonnez-moi*, madame," Rochelle Goyle called out in a charming Scarisian accent as she crested the building's front steps. "I do not wish to impose upon your business, but might you be looking for this?"

Rochelle bent down, picked up a raven-haired head with crimson lips, and handed it to the imposing headless figure standing next to the main doorway.

"Child, thank you! I keep forgetting my head, both figuratively and literally! You see, I was recently struck by lightning, and it's left me with a spot of what the doctor calls muddled mind. But not to worry, it won't last forever," Headmistress Bloodgood said upon remounting her head on her neck. "Now then, do I know you? In my current condition, I find it hard to remember faces or names or, if I am to be honest, almost anything."

"No, madame, you definitely do not know me. I am Rochelle Goyle from Scaris, and I shall be living in the new dormitory on campus."

"I am awfully thrilled that our reputation as the premier monster academy has attracted so many international students. You've come from Scaris, have you? However did you get here? I hope not atop the back of your sweet-faced griffin," Headmistress Bloodgood said while pointing to Rochelle's peppy little pet.

"Paragraph 11.5 of the Gargoyle Code of Ethics advises against sitting atop furniture, never mind pets! We came via Werewolf Hairlines, a most reliable company; the planes even come equipped

4

with reinforced steel seats for those of us made of stone," Rochelle said as she looked down at her slim but weighty figure. "Madame, might I bother you for directions to the dormitory?"

Before Headmistress Bloodgood could respond, however, Rochelle was thrown to the ground by what felt like a wall of water. Hard, damp, and extremely cold, an unknown entity instantly covered both Rochelle and Roux in a dense, misty fog. Looking up from the floor, she saw a short, rotund woman with gray hair storming through the crowd like a tsunami, knocking over everything within a five-foot radius.

"Miss Sue Nami?" Headmistress Bloodgood called out as the watery woman rammed an unsuspecting vampire into a wall.

Upon hearing Headmistress Bloodgood's high-pitched voice, Miss Sue Nami turned and stomped back, leaving a path of puddles in her wake. Up close, Rochelle couldn't help but notice the woman's permanently pruned skin, crisp blue eyes, and unflattering stance. With her legs a foot apart and her hands perched on her shapeless hips, the woman very much reminded Rochelle of a wrestler, albeit a male wrestler.

"Yes, ma'am?" Miss Sue Nami barked in a piercingly loud voice.

"This young lady is one of our new boarders, so would you mind showing her to the dormitory?" Headmistress Bloodgood asked Miss Sue Nami before turning back to Rochelle. "You are in good hands. Miss Sue Nami is the school's new Deputy of Disaster."

Fearing that students might take advantage of her temporary state of absentmindedness, especially where detentions in the dungeon were concerned, the headmistress had recently brought in Miss Sue Nami to handle all disciplinary matters.

"Nonadult entity, grab your bag and your toy and follow me," Miss Sue Nami screeched at Rochelle.

"Roux is not a toy but my pet griffin. I do not wish to mislead you—or anyone else, for that matter. Gargoyles take the truth very seriously."

"Lesson number one: When your mouth moves, you are talking. Lesson number two: When your legs move, you are walking. If you cannot do them simultaneously, then please focus only on the latter," Miss Sue Nami snapped before turning around and marching through the school's colossal front door.

Upon entering the hallowed halls of Monster High, Rochelle was instantly overwhelmed with a serious case of homesickness. Everything around her looked and felt terribly unfamiliar. She was used to lush fabric-covered walls, ornate gold-leafed moldings, and enormous crystal

7

chandeliers. But then again her last school, École de Gargouille, was housed in a chateau that was once the residence of the Count of Scaris. So, as one might expect, Rochelle was rather shocked by Monster High's modern purple-checkered floors, green walls, and pink coffin-shaped lockers. Not to mention the elaborately carved headstone, just inside the main doors, that reminded students it was against school policy to howl, molt fur, bolt limbs, or wake sleeping bats in the hallways.

"*Pardonnez-moi*, Miss Sue Nami, but are there really bats? As I am sure you know, bats can carry a wide variety of illnesses," Rochelle said. Her short gray legs worked overtime to keep up with the stampeding wet woman.

"Monster High employs vaccinated bats as in-house exterminators to eat rogue insects and spiders. With certain members of the student body bringing live insects for lunch, we consider

the bats highly regarded members of the janitorial staff. If you have a problem with them, I suggest you take it up with the headmistress. But I *highly* suggest confirming her head is properly attached before doing so," Miss Sue Nami grumbled as she rammed into an open door and, shortly thereafter, a slow-moving zombie.

The stunned zombie teetered sluggishly back and forth before collapsing to the ground, eliciting sympathetic whimpers from both Rochelle and Roux. Miss Sue Nami, however, stomped full speed ahead, totally oblivious to the effects of her reckless marching.

"I do not wish to tell you how to conduct your business, madame. But I must ask—are you aware that you have knocked quite a few monsters to the ground in the short time we have been walking?" Rochelle asked as tactfully as possible.

"That is known as collateral damage in the school-discipline business. Now, stop dawdling and pick up the pace; I'm on a schedule here!" Miss Sue Nami barked. "And if you are capable of both walking and listening, you will enjoy a brief tour along the way. If not, then I am merely reminding myself where everything is! On your immediate right, we have the Absolutely Deranged Scientist Laboratory, which is not to be confused with the Mad and Deranged Scientist Laboratory, currently under construction in the catacombs."

"Isn't that going to be unnecessarily confusing?" Rochelle wondered aloud as she glanced into the room filled with Bunsen burners, vials of colorful liquids, plastic safety goggles, white lab coats, and countless peculiar-looking apparatuses.

"I have decided to disregard your question, as I do not deem it relevant. I will now continue with my tour. The laboratory is currently being used for Mad Science class, in which students produce a wide variety of things, such as lotion for the scaly-skinned, antifungal drops for the pumpkin heads, fur-calming serum for the hairy, organic oil for the robotically inclined, industrial-strength mouthwash for the sea monsters, and much more," Miss Sue Nami explained before stopping to shake her body like a dog after a bath, spraying everyone in a three-foot radius with water. Fortunately, as gargoyles are built to deflect water, both Rochelle and her dress were spared.

"I love water, and even *I* think that was super gross," a scaly-skinned sea creature dressed in flip-flops and well-tailored fluorescent-pink board shorts muttered while she wiped her face with a fishnet scarf.

"Well, at least you don't have a fur 'fro now," a stylishly clad werewolf moaned, touching her long and luscious mane of now wet auburn hair.

"Lagoona Blue, Clawdeen Wolf, do not waste your lives standing around in the hallway complaining. Go and complain in private, like the smart, ambitious monsters you are."

"*Bonjour*," Rochelle mumbled quietly, offering

a painfully awkward smile to Lagoona and Clawdeen.

"A Scaremès scarf as a belt? That's straight out of *Morgue Magazine*! Totally creeperific," Clawdeen complimented her, clearly impressed by Rochelle's chic style.

"*Merci boo-coup*," the gargoyle called out as she jetted after the fast-moving Miss Sue Nami.

"Next we have the bell tower, just behind which you will find the courtyard and the Creepateria, respectively. To your immediate left you have the gym, the Casketball Court, Study Howl, and finally the Creepchen, where Home Ick is taught," Miss Sue Nami said rapidly while storming through the cavernous purple-and-green halls.

After banging into a row of pink coffin-shaped lockers, the puddle-prone woman turned down an adjoining corridor and quickly resumed her tour guide duties.

"Here we have the graveyard, where you can fulfill your Physical Deaducation requirement with Graveyard Dancing, but of course you can also do that by joining the Skulltimate Roller Maze team, which practices next door in the maze. Next we have the dungeon, where detention is held, and finally the Libury, where both Ghoulish Literature and Monstory: The History of Monsters are taught."

"Would it be possible to get a map?" Rochelle inquired politely with Roux perched sweetly on her shoulder. "While I have a most remarkable brain for remembering things, I'm all rocks and pebbles when it comes to directions."

"Maps are for people who are afraid to get lost, or lost people who are afraid to get found, neither of which applies to you. Plus, for the time being all you really need to know is where the Vampitheater is, for the start-of-the-term assembly."

SCHOOL OF FEAR

Sharpen your pencils and put on a brave face.
The School of Fear is waiting for YOU!
Will you banish your fears and graduate on time?

IT'S NEVER TOO LATE TO APPLY!

www.EnrollinSchoolofFear.com

Don't miss these defrightful activity journals for ghouls!

Available now!